Postmark PARIS

Destination UNKNOWN

A Novel

by

Gary Paul Corcoran

Published by Stargazer Press
Charlestown, Rhode Island

This is a work of fiction. Names, characters, organizations, places, events and incidents are either products of the author's imagination or are used fictitiously. Any similarity to persons living or dead is merely coincidental.

Printed in the United States of America
ISBN: 978-0-9971265-4-9

Visit us and blog with the author at
http://garypaulcorcoran.com/

Acknowledgements

Michael, as always, for an exquisite cover, Eric, for the unanticipated loan that helped me cross the pond, the boys in the Citroën, who shared a simple kindness with this wayward young man along the road of life, the same of the winemakers wife, who carried me off to the Alps, and David and Captain Hook and the British gal with the sun splashed cottage, to the boys in Milan and all the French, German, Spanish and Italian ladies of the world, and the many, many other kind souls who turned what could have been a wretched trip into a magical journey.

Thank you. You are all forever in my heart.

For Kimberly,
Who shared so much of her heart.
Thank you for all those kindnesses,
and for encouraging me to tell this story...

"Bliss it was in that dawn to be alive
But to be young was very heaven."

William Wordsworth

March 29, 2011

All these years later and I still cannot properly explain what made me do it. Love, of course. Romance. L'amour. Why else would a man cast his fate to the wind the way I did? Yet somehow that fails to answer the question, and hardly matters, for we are missing the point; that I sit here today, lo these many years later, remembering little of what I thought would bring me security and safekeeping in this world, or the many doors I have opened, the light switches I have turned on or off, the countless bills I have paid and hallways I have wandered down. But that great adventure? Now that I remember as if it were yesterday…and would do it all over again…at the drop of a hat. I remember too that day so long ago, sitting in Signore Gabriele's Italian villa, and how, in speaking of his own youthful adventures, he had tried to warn me, that if he had one regret in this world, it was that he had abandoned his dreams and come running home far too soon.

The final entry from a journal found among Paul Daly's papers following his untimely death…

One

I had come to be living high up on a hill that spring, overlooking a sylvan valley that had cradled much my youth and where I had journeyed from the days of boyhood into being a man. This was well before the new tract homes and freeway began to go in; when the valley was still very much an untamed thing, with a wild river running through it and farmhouses dotting the countryside and an old two-lane highway winding its way east out towards the coastal mountains and deserts beyond. At night, you could see the headlights coming and going along the darkened roads and the lights of homesteads flicker here and there in the valley and I was always very content to be high up in that place, with that fine view of the world and a majestic oak tree towering over my humble abode.

My nightly routine upon arriving home was to back my Peugeot up under the oak tree, slide the front seats forward and fold them down—which the French in their ingenious manner had designed to make into a completely flat bed—then gather my pillows and blankets and foam pad from the trunk and make myself comfortable for the night. I had a one burner Coleman stove for brewing up coffee in the mornings or for warming up the occasional meal at night but I worked as a cook and took the bulk of my meals at the restaurant or at various eateries around town. I had marveled at the time and still marvel to this day that I never saw one other soul up there on that knoll, night or day, despite the existence of a nearby rock quarry and a road accessing it that ran right past my hilltop home.

My girlfriend Eva often joined me on weekend nights and on those occasions you would find us lying together under the covers and gazing up at the stars through my open sunroof. Eva came from a rich family and was going off to college in the fall and her parents had little use for me as an aimless young man. I, in turn, had little use for them but had not troubled myself much beyond that when it came to our predictable differences. As is common with most men of eighteen, I loved blindly and with an assumption on some level that Eva and I would be together forever and ever, or at least for the rest of our lives.

I was without question a rebellious soul — though I firmly believed with good cause — had dropped out of high school in my senior year and otherwise had no idea what to make of myself. Following a bloody fistfight with my old man one night, I had gone out to sit in my Peugeot when my mother appeared, tearful and telling me that I had to go. It was time for the cub to leave the den. I would now have to face the world all on my own.

Eva was in her senior year at an all-girls Catholic high school and with graduation drawing near, her every thought had been to finish in the top fifty students, thereby qualifying for a school sponsored tour of Europe. Given her family's abundant resources, and the fact that the tour would be chaperoned by nuns, I had never understood Eva's zeal for the whole affair, but she was determined and had received word a few weeks earlier that she had made the cut.

Our plan was to attend her high school prom that Friday night, then Eva would be off to Europe on Monday morning. I ached quite a bit over her impending departure and often dreamed of ways to tag along on the trip but travelling abroad like that was way beyond my means.

At the time, I was working dinner prep at a local steak house and drove over to visit Eva at her dorm room that Wednesday night after work. Her room was in a wing of the Catholic school, on the floor above a row of classrooms, and since boys weren't allowed anywhere near the place, except on formal occasions, the only way into her dorm room was to crawl up through her second story window.

Having parked one street below the school, I made my way up a hill through a thicket of eucalyptus trees and oleanders and threw the obligatory pebble at Eva's window. Moments later, she opened it, waved and dropped a rope down that had been tied to the legs of an old wall heater inside.

While shimmying my way up the brick building, I heard Eva's friends whispering and giggling and Eva admonishing them to keep quiet. Once at the window level, I gripped the ledge and pulled myself into the candle lit room. Eva gave me a kiss and pulled the rope back up inside.

"Did you get it?" Leslie whispered.

"Yeah," I said and settled onto the floor at the foot of Eva's bed.

The chunk of hashish came out, along with a small pipe. The women gathered around me as I loaded the bowl, took the first hit and passed the pipe to Eva. All four women were soon choking back coughs.

Time passed, the drug took effect and Leslie and Beth began joking around in the candlelit room. Eva had to shush them again. Then Beth noticed me staring at her and made eyes.

"What, Paul?"

"Oh…you're just looking all archetypal all of a sudden."

"What kind of archetypal?"

"Like a Flamenco dancer, maybe."

Delighting in her role, the dark-haired and dark eyed Beth sprang to her feet and commenced a passionate dance with pretend castanets. Then the tall and willowy Leslie was on her feet, her strawberry blonde hair swaying all about as she tossed pretend flower petals upon the world.

"Let me guess. I'm the fairy maiden of spring."

"That would be you," I said.

Eva looked to the heavens.

"Who am I?" Tanya said.

Beth stopped in her tracks.

"Dia de los muertos in the flesh."

"You know what? Fuck you."

"Well? It's been boo hoo hoo ever since John broke up with you."

"Well, what would you do if your boyfriend dumped you for one of your friends? Have a big laugh?"

"No. I'd find someone new. *And* some new friends. Anyway, John's a jerk and we'll be in in Europe in less than a week. Think of all the French and Italian and Spanish hunks we'll have to choose from."

"Hunks," Leslie repeated.

"Hmmmmm," Beth said.

Eva looked to the heavens again. Beth and Leslie settled back onto the floor.

"Sorry," Beth said to me.

"Sorry about what?"

"About the hunks."

"What do I care? I'm an Irish/Italian hunk."

"Hmm. You are."

Eva kicked her.

Tanya sat there staring at the floor, looking miserable. Time had not been kind to her. At thirteen, she had been cherubic. Now, four years later, her pubescent beauty was mostly spent, her flat face having grown broad, her short, compact body now stout with bowled legs.

I looked at Eva. She was the princess of the lot, proud in bearing, with silky blonde hair and blue-green eyes the color of a summer sky at twilight. They sparkled in the darkness like the first evening star.

"What?" I said to Beth, seeing her stare at me.

"Oh, I was just thinking, why don't you come to Europe with us?"

"Yeah! We'll sneak you onto the plane!" Leslie said.

"Sure, I'll go in drag."

That got them to giggling.

"Or, I know, as a nun," Beth said.

"My, but what strange muscles you have, Sister Daly."

Beth and Leslie went on and on with their absurd scheme, and I felt lousier and lousier, listening to them. As a young man, I too wanted to go off and see the world. Every time I thought of Europe, I thought of my childhood dream, soaring over Bavarian villages and castles far below me. I hated that Eva got to go off on her big adventure while I was left behind.

"Hey, did any of you hear *Give Peace a Chance* on the radio today?" Leslie asked.

Both Beth and Eva shook their heads. I nodded.

"I heard it too," Tanya said. "Lennon's so cool."

"Yeah," Leslie said.

Tanya joined Leslie in whispering the chorus.

"Keep it down," Eva said.

"Is it just a single or a new album?" Beth said.

"I guess it's going to be on his new album," Leslie said. "But they're not releasing it for another month or so they just wanted to get the single out there for the antiwar movement this summer."

Beth now joined Tanya and Leslie in whispering the chorus.

"All we are saying is give peace a chance."

Hearing talk of peace, my thoughts turned to the war. It was the madness behind all the other madness in the world. Not all that long ago, our generation had been giddy with youthful dreams, but that innocence had been blown away year by year—and the current year wasn't turning out to be much better.

I looked up to find Leslie staring at me now.

"Why are you always so serious?" she asked.

"Why are you always so chirpy?"

She shoved me playfully.

"Come on. Answer my question. I never see you smiling."

"Well? If you knew you were heading over to get killed in Vietnam next year, wouldn't you be on a bummer?"

"But you don't know that. You might not even get drafted."

"Well let's just say the prospect of it's enough to get me down."

"So you're going to be on a downer for another year."

"I don't know. Maybe longer. I'll have to get back to you."

She shoved me again and got back to chirping away with Beth. Everything was a gag to them.

I sat there half listening, my thoughts still hung up on the war. I would find my mind going around and around about it for days. And the men behind it. I could dwell on it all for days on end.

Leslie was right though. I might not get drafted. I just knew my name would be entered into the lottery the following year and that if my number came up, I'd have to choose; go fight in 'Nam, come up with a deferment or head to Canada. The war showed no signs of ending soon. It was impossible not to be concerned.

Eva, who had been fingering my long hair while lost in thought, suddenly spoke up.

"Did you get the tux?"

I looked into her sparkling, blue-green eyes. The hunters of the heart, a troubadour had once said, and Eva's eyes slayed me like no others. I hardly understood my ardor for her. I only knew that I was in love with a woman, as much as a young man can be.

"Yeah, I got it."

"Where?"

"In a box in my trunk."

"I want to see it."

"Well then, let's just slither down that rope and go have a look."

Beth and Leslie snickered. Eva gave me a sly smile.

"Did you try it on?"

"Of course. That's why you go there."

"So? How did it fit?"

"Fine."

Eva picked at my collar.

"You're sure?"

I nodded. She brushed at my hair.

"And you got the blue one?"

"Yeah, the blue one, just like you said."

"With the black tie?"

"Oh shoot. I thought you wanted the one with purple polka dots."

Beth and Leslie cracked up. I glanced over at them. Their painted toenails were getting a workout.

"Why do you always have to be so smart?" Eva said.

I shrugged. I figured it was just a young woman wanting a young man's attention, but sometimes her questions really did get under my skin.

With a pause in the room, I grabbed the hash pipe.

"What do you say to another bowl, ladies?"

That was met with approvals all around.

The next morning, before heading off to work, I stopped by my friend Tim's place to take a shower. His parents owned a big ranch house with several acres a mile or so down the valley from my place and both of them had gone off to their day jobs.

While showering, I had thoughts of Tim and all my friends dashing excitedly about campus during the last week of high school. Yearbooks signed. Summer memories planned. Plaster caps tossed into the air. I wanted to pretend that I didn't care about all that crap, but somewhere deep down inside of me, I did.

Then I remembered Eva's trip and tried to put all of it out of my mind.

That Friday night, I drove over to pick up Eva at her parent's house. It was a spacious, Frank Lloyd Wright looking thing in a tony neighborhood. They could have afforded a castle, so by that standard, it was fairly modest.

"Oh, hi Paul," her mother said in answering the door. "Please come in."

She opened the door wide and closed it behind me.

"You're looking nice."

"Thanks."

She had said it without the least bit of emotion.

"Go ahead and have a seat. Eva will be out in a moment."

Mrs. Gabriele disappeared. I sat on a stiff but very expensive sofa.

Eva appeared a few minutes later with her hair pinned up and smelling of roses. Mrs. Gabriele joined us with a camera and took several photos. Then Eva and I were out the door and off to the prom. Mrs. Gabriele watched from the front door as we drove off in my old Peugeot.

Eva's Catholic school had arranged the prom at a hotel down by the waterfront. The hotel itself was nice. The banquet room was a big, cavernous box and the food was tasteless. The waiters came around with a metal lid over your plate and said 'voila' while revealing the meal. I had roast beef that chewed like old leather.

Eva and I danced long enough to put on a front and then ran off to a big party up at Tim's place. Tim's parents had gone off for the weekend and their sprawling ranch house was a madhouse.

At the first opportunity, Eva and I snuck off to make love in his parent's bedroom. A chart of some kind had been tacked to the wall next to their bed, with X's marked on it here and there.

"What the hell is that?" I said.

"It's to keep track of her ovulation cycle." Eva said. "The X's mark the best days for her to get pregnant."

"So that's when they *did* it," I said.

"Yeah. They must be strict Catholics."

"Yeah, well. What do you say we get down to a bit of the old X's and O's, sweetheart?"

Eva slapped at me and asked me to unzip her gown. The chart loomed over our enterprise. You couldn't help but have visions of American Gothic; pitchforks and the likes.

On Monday morning, Eva flew off to New York and Europe. Through the grapevine, I heard that Tim's parents had learned of our mischief and burned their mattress or something of that sort.

Whatever had gone down, I was forever banned from their house. Even Tim was pissed and I heard his older brother Richard was out looking for me.

Tired of the old scene anyway, I drove down to the beach and looked for work. Jobs as a cook were a dime a dozen along that row of waterfront dives and restaurants.

With a new job in hand, I rented a clapboard cottage over on the rough and tumble side of the back bay. It was one of ten cottages arranged in a u-shape configuration. Parking was in potholed dirt lot in front of the cottages. Probably the place had been a quaint little beach destination back in the day. Now it was grim. The rent was cheap. The residents called it Tobacco Road.

One of my coworkers Mark invited me out for a pitcher of beer that first night after work and I started running with him and his gang. Dreams of Eva and Europe filled my days but I did my best not to get too down about being left back home.

Two

A week or so after Eva's departure, I received a letter, postmarked from Rome. In it, Eva chirped on and on about all the fun she was having. She would write again once the tour had reached Madrid. That would be in three days.

The letter was signed...Love, Eva. Not a word was said about having missed me.

I looked towards the horizon, longing for my own great adventure. I knew it was out there, somewhere, across the Seven Seas.

That Saturday, my friends and I headed over the coastal hills, on our way to a love-in. The vast plain beyond the hills was primarily used for agriculture. We saw the occasional feed place and country store and then passed through miles and miles of orange groves with rows of eucalyptus trees towering over the road. The groves and farmland together represented the remnants of huge land grants doled out by King Phillip to his conquering soldiers.

Rolling hills girded the horizon. Hawks circled in the sky and horses grazed alongside split-rail fences. One of our friends had stood up through the sunroof, shouting into the wind as we motored along.

The love-in was being held on an abandoned drag strip with the stage set up at one end of the runway. People spilled out into the surrounding meadows and the mood was generally festive under the hot summer sun.

We ran into two guys with a magic bus, parked at the opposite end of the runway. They called themselves Batman and Robin. I had no idea why. I guess because they were a duo. With their long hair and beards and tie dye clothing, they were not your typical super heroes.

Batman and Robin had installed a barber's chair in the back of their bus and people took turns having a hit of the herb then being spun around at high speed. By the time the chair came to a stop, you had no idea where you were.

Late that afternoon, we left the revelry behind and made our way back to Tobacco Road. One of my new neighbors and two of his buddies popped into my cottage a few minutes after we had arrived.

"Check this out," he said and held up a flight mask rigged to a water pipe. "For turbo charging hits."

I gave him my tentative blessing and continued on to retrieve a beer from the refrigerator. A minute later, someone was escaping out from under the flight mask with a gasp. The entire cottage had grown thick with smoke. I sat back in a corner, not entirely comfortable with all these people crammed into my little space. There was a feeling of things getting out of control.

Eventually, I put an end to the flight mask business and was fanning at the smoke when someone knocked loudly on my door. Panic swept through the cottage. You had to think it was the cops.

Following a scramble to get all the paraphernalia safely tucked away, and having cleared the air a bit more, I cracked the door. A Western Union delivery boy stood on my front porch.

"Yeah?" I said

"I have a telegram for Paul Daly. From Madrid."

Assuming it was from Eva, I pulled out my ID and signed on the dotted line. The delivery boy hurried back to his car. I closed the door.

"He probably thinks we're some kind of cult," Mark said.

"We probably are," someone else said to much laughter.

I opened the telegram and stood there in shock.

In Madrid. Stop. Leaving tomorrow for Barcelona. Stop. Reach Paris June 30. Stop. I'm pregnant. Stop.

I read the telegram several more times, unable to believe my own eyes.

"What?" someone said.

Mark grabbed the telegram from my hands and cracked up.

"Wow, his chick's pregnant."

The telegram got passed around the room to more laughs.

"Oh man. Now you're really going to have to go hide out in Canada."

"Yeah, man. Who wants a kid?"

"Here, have another hit, brother."

I did and stood there in disbelief.

Pregnant. Paris. June 30th.

Those three things kept going around and around in my head.

"So what are you going to do, man?" Mark asked me.

I had no idea. Eva's parents would never allow her to have a child, especially not one by me. However, she did have a rich uncle in Turin, who disliked them as much as I did. It figured that if I could get Eva to Turin, everything else would fall into place—a roof over our heads, a job, a future.

Amidst the ongoing gags about Eva and me starting a family, my mind went to work on a plan. Eva's tour was scheduled to land in Paris on June 30th, then depart for London on July 3rd. After that, she would be heading home. That gave me roughly two weeks to intercept her and pull off the mission, and my only hope of accomplishing that goal was to quit my job, collect my last paycheck and sell my car. I'd be nearly broke by the time I got to Europe but things would have to work themselves out from there.

In a matter of minutes, my heart had galloped off to rescue my fair princess.

I went into work the next morning and gave my boss the news. He was pissed about the lack of advance notice but reluctantly wrote out a check. I immediately cashed it and drove up to LA to apply for a passport. The usual wait time was six weeks, but for an extra fifty bucks they could expedite the process down to a week. I gave them the money and headed over to San Pedro, thinking there had to be a cheaper way of reaching Europe. The idea of landing in Paris nearly broke and with no return ticket seemed like madness, even to me.

I arrived at the harbor and parked in an open lot. Much wandering followed. So did dreams of the Sargasso Sea.

By chance, I ran into an off duty sailor and was guided over to the merchant marine office. Inside, I asked how much it would cost to get my papers and how soon I could get out on a ship. It was two hundred dollars to join, a few weeks to get my papers and then I'd be on a long waiting list. I could be sitting around for months before shipping out.

Seeing it was a dead end, I went outside and wandered back among the docks. Massive ships towered over me, their hulls seeping rusty bilge water like blood.

Four British sailors standing high up on the causeway of their freighter saw me approach and waved hello.

"Looking to get shanghaied, mate?" one of them called down.

I stared up. They seemed friendly enough so I explained the situation.

"Must be some bird," one of them said.

"Yeah. So you think maybe there's some way I could work my way over to Europe?"

They talked among themselves and looked back.

"We could probably stow you away among the potatoes, if you'd like."

They seemed to be entirely sincere, as crazy as it sounded.

"How long would it take to get to Europe?"

They looked at each other and shrugged.

"With the trip through the canal and all, a bit more than two weeks."

Hell. Another dead end. I knew if I didn't catch up with Eva in Paris, all would be lost. At best I'd have an extra day to reach her in London.

Thanking the sailors, I headed back to my car. There was no other choice. Sell the Peugeot, fly to New York and look for the cheapest way to Europe. If I arrived in Paris broke, so be it. Once Eva and I made our way to Turin and her rich uncle, things would be fine.

I sent Eva a telegram, informing her of my plans. I would arrive in Paris the evening of July 1, July 2nd at the latest. I then set about arranging things for the trip. Knowing there was always the unexpected, I bought a backpack, a sleeping bag and a bit of camping gear. I had a pair of Spanish boots to wear and a beaded satchel from Morocco. As an afterthought, I located a pawn shop and purchased an old camera.

Arriving home that afternoon, I found a notice from Western Union tacked to my door, marked urgent. Figuring the telegram was from Eva, I drove directly over to their office and retrieved it.

In a few words, Eva made her intentions clear.

> Everything's fine. Stop. Don't come. Stop. Will explain when I get home. Stop.

I sent her a return telegram. It was already arranged. Expect to see me as planned.

While waiting for my passport, I bought a ticket to New York, flying out the following Sunday, and arranged to sell my car to an old friend Steve. That next Thursday, I called the consulate in LA, learned my passport was ready and drove up on Friday morning. The remainder of that day and Saturday was spent tying up loose ends.

On Sunday evening, I drove over to drop off the car with Steve. As part of the deal, he had agreed to drive me up to the airport. Steve and several of our friends were sitting around a darkened living room, smoking dope and talking about how they were going to go live out in the country. Last year it had been all about bringing down the government. Now everyone was looking for someplace to hide.

I sat down next to Steve on the sofa. He took a big hit, coughed and handed me the joint.

"I hope you're not bummed but I'm a hundred dollars short in cash."

"What the hell, Steve? We had everything arranged."

"I know, man but I ran out of grass and came across this really good shit."

He showed me a big baggie full of it.

"You can have some if you want."

"What am I going to do with it? Barter at the airport for a ticket?"

That got a big laugh. I wasn't amused.

"I can write you a check for the difference," he said.

"A check? What am I going to do with a check? Cash it in Paris? 'Like trust me, man. Steve's a really good friend of mine'."

Everyone cracked up again. I wanted to kill Steve. There we were on a hot summer evening, with my plane scheduled to depart in three hours and no time to fix things.

"All right. Write me the goddamned check, you bastard."

I had another hit off the joint, beside myself.

"Come on," I said while they were still screwing around. "Let's go before I get a gun."

I stood up. Steve had one last hit and stood up with me. Another one of our friends decided to join us and we headed out the door.

Along the way the way to the airport, my head went around and around about the money. With the extra hundred dollars, things were already going to be tight. Without it, I wasn't sure I would be able to cover the ticket. Fear and excitement did battle in my heart. One way or the other, I was headed to Europe.

The redeye to New York turned out to be a mostly empty flight. There were almost as many stewardesses on the plane as passengers. I was able to stretch out across three seats and get some sleep.

We arrived to JFK and a packed terminal at eight in the morning. I quickly checked the international carriers and learned that a prop jet to Luxembourg with Lufthansa was my only option. It had a flight time of roughly twelve hours and a stopover in Iceland.

I booked the flight and did a final check on my finances. I would be arriving to the continent with Steve's check, ten dollars in cash and no return ticket.

I headed off to get some fresh air in front of the terminal, unaware that New York was in the grip of a heatwave. The heat and smog and humidity slapped me in the face as the glass door opened. First thing in the morning and it was already in the nineties.

I went right back inside and sat in a plastic chair, for the first time questioning my headlong adventure. Ten dollars in cash, a hundred dollar, two-party check and no return ticket? I had to be crazy. Eva had told me to wait. Maybe it would be best if I cashed in the ticket and headed back to the west coast.

I wandered up to the boarding area anyway and found a scene straight out of Haight-Ashbury. Freaks with guitars. Women in tie-dye blouses. Hair and headbands and beads everywhere you looked.

While I sat there, a woman's voice came over the intercom. Flight 497, now boarding at gate 35 for London. That got my blood stirring again. The big wide world was out there, on the next flight taking off.

Every few minutes, the woman's voice announced another departure. Then it was time for our plane to board. I got in line, my uncertainties dragged forward by nebulous hopes and dreams.

Onboard the plane, things quickly turned to pandemonium. People were singing and laughing and banging on tambourines. The stewardesses tried to get everyone under control and finally gave up.

Our pilot came over the intercom and announced that he was diverting us up to Nova Scotia for a refueling stop. It was too dangerous to take off with a full load of fuel in this heat wave.

As soon as were in the air and the seatbelt sign went off, there were joints being passed around and people dancing in the aisles. The guy sitting in the next seat took a hit and handed me the joint.

"Far out scene, huh?" he said.

"Yeah, a trip."

I took a hit and passed the joint to the next guy. My mind was a million miles away. While my generation was staging a love-in at 30,000 feet, I was Tristan off to save Iseult. A knight on his grave mission.

Roughly an hour later, we landed in Nova Scotia. Then we were off to Iceland. The party kept going.

When we touched down in Reykjavik, I went outside to get some fresh air. After New York, the coolness was a relief.

A guy in full Green Beret regalia came out, lit up a cigarette nearby and leaned over the railing.

"Want one?" he said.

I shook my head.

"Wild trip, huh?" he said.

I nodded.

"Where are you headed?" he asked.

I told him. He laughed.

"You're daring. I'll give you that much."

"Yeah. I'm guessing most people would call me crazy."

He laughed again and dug out a card.

"Here. If you're ever near Ramstein, look me up. I'll put you up for free."

"Thanks."

With a look at the card, I stuck it in my pocket. Hippies and people in the military rarely mingled in those days, and I doubted I'd ever be in Ramstein, but he was a kind soul to offer his help. I waited until he had finished his cigarette and joined him back inside.

We were there on the ground for about an hour before taking off again. With the extra stop in Nova Scotia, the flight was turning into a sixteen hour marathon.

The remaining leg to Luxembourg was considerably more subdued. Night fell along the way and people in general tried to get some sleep. All I could think of was Eva. In less than twelve hours, she would be in my arms. That assumed she was still in Paris. Any number of things could have happened since our last communication.

All the while, a vibration rumbled down the length of the plane, back and forth, back and forth, over and over as I tried to find sleep.

At dawn I awakened to a view of the Belgium countryside far below my window. I stared down, reminded again of my childhood dreams, soaring over hill and dale and castle. Only now it was for real, not a boy awakening to find his dreams dissolving into the walls of suburbia.

As we disembarked onto the tarmac, my emotions were all over the place. Would I find Eva? Would she come with me? Would things work out with her uncle? And how would I survive if all my plans went up in smoke? I had no idea but my heart was beating wildly.

Postmark
PARIS
Destination
UNKNOWN
A Novel

Three

The circus of earth mothers and traveling minstrels filed down to the tarmac and inside to the customs area in a buzz of ongoing conversation and laughter. A row of agents in navy-blue uniforms sat behind windows framed with dark wood, awaiting as we queued up. The line inched slowly forward.

Some minutes later, I was standing before an older gentleman with thinning hair combed straight back. He greeted me formally and asked to see my passport. Having quickly thumbed through the unstamped pages, he asked to see my backpack. I set it up on the counter and shoved it through the opening. While making a cursory search inside, he asked me a few more questions.

Where was I coming from? Where was I going? And how long did I plan to stay? Remarkably, he never asked to see how much money I had or if I possessed a return ticket.

With a perfunctory stamp of my passport, I was welcomed to Luxembourg and the next person in line was waved up to the window.

On my way out of the terminal, I noticed a tourist office and went in to inquire about cashing the check. My French was nearly fluent but the female agent quickly turned to English and asked to see my check. She then did a directory search and located a Bank of America branch in Paris. It might take a few days to clear the funds but they would likely cash it for me.

I thanked her and went out to the loading zone in front. It was getting on into mid-morning and the summer day was already hot. There were forested hills across from the airport. The sky was clear save for a few high clouds.

How to get to Paris? That was the question. Given my state of penury, hitchhiking was the only realistic option. The ten dollars in cash might buy me a train or bus fare, but then I would be completely broke until I cashed the check. And that assumed I could cash it.

I had been standing in front of the terminal with my map for a minute, considering how best to get out to the highway when an old black Citroën pulled up to the curb. A picture of Mr. Mxyztplk had been painted on the front door — bald head, purple suit, green bow tie and all — along with his name in white paint. Klptzyxm was spelled out below this, the magic word that made him disappear. On the back door there was an image of Snoopy as the Red Baron, with a red scarf.

Two young men piled out of the Citroën and offered a hale and hearty hello to a young man standing near me. He had been on the same Lufthansa flight.

With their conversation ongoing, the man's luggage was tossed in the trunk and all three of them climbed back into the

Citroën. The driver started the car, crunched the transmission into gear and lurched forward. I stared after them.

A few feet farther on, the driver hit the brakes, backed up and leaned over in order to see me through the passenger side window.

"Did you need a ride somewhere?"

"Depends on where you're headed."

"Where are you headed?"

"I'm trying to get to Paris."

With a shrug at his two companions, he turned off the car and they all climbed back out.

"Douglas," the man driving said and shook my hand. "Charles and Andrew."

I shook their hands too.

"Let's see your map."

We spread it out across the hood. They were headed north for the coast through Amiens and had intended to turn off at Reims, but it wouldn't be too much of an inconvenience for them to turn north at Meaux instead. It wasn't Paris, but it was a hell of a lot closer. I could catch a local bus from there.

"Groovy?" Douglas said to me.

"Yeah, man. Totally groovy. Thanks."

I placed my pack in their trunk and climbed into the backseat with Charles. Douglas started the car, crunched it back into gear and drove off.

The way south led alternately up through forested hills and down through rolling farmland. All the while, we passed around a bottle of red wine and talked of life and of our differing adventures. The three of them had just graduated from Princeton and were spending the summer in Europe together before returning for their graduate work in the fall. Douglas was staying at Princeton. Charles was going on to Yale, Andrew to Harvard.

Having dropped out of high school, I had no such patrician story to tell. Princeton? Ivy League? I'd be lucky to get into a junior college. Headlong adventures was my current major.

I explained what had brought me to Europe and that got a lot of wows. Then the conversation grew silent and I dug out my map. Charles glanced my way with a smile.

"You know, this was one of Hitler's favorite routes."

"Oh, he was always big on the scenic," Andrew said from the front.

Douglas laughed.

"Sure, he'd go anywhere for a good croissant and espresso."

Douglas glanced at me.

"What do you say, Paul?"

"I guess any man could grow tired of German strudel."

Douglas did a double take over the seat and burst out laughing.

"Good one, good one," Charles said.

"Hey, I wouldn't mind a little German strudel right about now," Andrew said.

Douglas made up a Bavarian sounding song involving German strudels and we all sang along.

Up and down we went, through forest and alongside rolling wheat fields swaying in the summer sun. In one village we stopped to buy a loaf of bread, some cheese and another bottle of wine and passed them around, telling more stories, and soon the morning had passed into late afternoon.

When we reached the outskirts of Meaux, my companions turned right at the crossroads and bid me farewell. I watched their car disappear and walked up to a bus stop. Paris was yet a dream on the horizon, some twenty miles away, but I could already imagine its dusky cafés and lovers kissing on street corners and chestnut trees whispering in the summer breeze. I sat there waiting with the scent of diesel fumes filling the air.

A bus eventually came along and I boarded it. Charles had traded my dollars for francs in the backseat and I used those to pay the fare.

The bus left Meaux behind and entered open country again. Buildings dotted the roadside here and there but for the most part it remained farmland. Then, little by little, commerce grew up around us, with side streets radiating out increasingly from the main road. Then the outskirts of Paris had swallowed the horizon.

We entered the city at dusk, with waiters in white shirts and black pants getting sidewalk cafés ready for the evening. I saw two of them unstacking tables and chairs and snapping open tablecloths. A young couple passed by in the twilight and both waiters stopped to stare at the woman.

Paris went on for miles and miles and I had to change buses three times, but with each stop I drew ever closer to the Hôtel Américain. The last bus driver dropped me off across the street from the hotel. It was almost as wide as it was tall and utterly drab in its rigid, mid-century geometry.

I dashed through passing traffic and a doorman opened the front door for me. Inside, I quickly located the concierge and explained my reason for being there. My French being what it was, I was treated with the commensurate respect and directed up to the fifth floor. I took the elevator and found Eva's room number halfway down a long hallway. When I knocked, I heard her voice call out from inside.

"Who's there?"

"Paul."

There were screams.

A moment later, the door opened and Eva stood before me, her blonde hair pinned up on her head and her blue-green eyes sparkling in the dusky light. Tanya, Beth and Leslie were curled up on the bed behind her, whispering excitedly among themselves. I could see at a glance that Tanya's mood had improved greatly with the trip.

I waved to them and kissed Eva.

"What are you doing?!" she whispered.

"What do you mean?" I whispered back. "I told you I was coming."

"You're crazy."

"What? I love you. I came to make things right."

"You're crazy," she said again. "I told you to wait."

"I know, but I'm here so let's talk about our plans."

"Later," she whispered and pulled on my arm. "Come inside."

Eva looked up and down the hallway before closing the door. The other three women fell silent as I approached the bed. Something was in the air and I was getting ready to ask exactly what that was but Beth jumped up from the bed and gave me a hug.

"Wow! I can't believe you actually made it!"

I put my pack down and hugged Leslie and Tanya in turn. The three of them were quickly curled back up on the bed with their silent stares. Curious, I went to the window and looked down at the traffic rushing by on the street.

"So, tell us about it!" Leslie said. "How did you get here?"

I sat in a wingback chair by the window. Eva sat on the arm next to me. I explained the journey without going into every little detail. The salient facts were, I had ten dollars in cash, a hundred dollar, two-party check and no return ticket. Understandably, everyone who had heard the story fixated on those three facts.

"So, how are you going to get home?" Tanya said.

"Who said I'm going home?" I glanced at Eva. "The first thing I need to do is find that Bank of America so I can cash this check and we'll go from there."

"We know where it is," Tanya said.

"It's right off the Champs-Élysées," Eva said with her fingers in my hair. "Next to the Western Union office."

"All the young people go there in the mornings so they can collect their dough from home," Leslie added with mock sarcasm.

"Cool," I said.

"So are you going out with us tonight?" Tanya said.

"I hope so. I came this far."

"Yay!" Beth said. "We're going to see Montmartre!"

"Montmartre," Leslie said with a heavy French accent.

Beth then said Montmartre with an even heavier accent and Leslie one upped her and the two of them went on riffing away on the theme.

"Montmarrrtre…"

"No, Montmarrrrrtre…"

No, no. Montmarrrrrrrrrtre."

They were close to choking.

"I think he gets the idea," Eva said.

Leslie threw a pillow at her.

"God! I still can't believe you're here!" Beth said.

"Me either."

Everyone laughed but Eva. I looked at her. Something unspoken lingered in that dusky room. Something didn't add up. I could smell it and see it in all of their eyes.

"Hey, well, I guess we'll leave you two alone for a while," Beth said and got up from the bed. Leslie and Tanya followed.

"We'll see you in a bit," Leslie added at the door.

She winked before closing it. I listened to their giggles and whispered conversation fade down the hallway and turned back to Eva.

"You shouldn't have come," she said.

"What do you mean? You sent me a telegram, telling me you were pregnant. What was I supposed to do?"

"I know. I thought you should know. Then I realized I should have waited…"

"Well, it's done now and I'm the father, so what are we going to do?"

"Well, that's why I sent you another telegram, telling you to wait. I had a miscarriage in Madrid."

"What are you talking about? You were only pregnant for what? Less than two months?"

"Well, it happens. I looked it up and it's pretty common with first time pregnancies."

Eva went on to explain how the fetus had come out stillborn while she was on the toilet and she had to flush it away.

"I was going to explain everything when I got back home."

I wasn't buying it.

"What would cause you to have a miscarriage?"

"I don't know. We were thinking maybe because we had to go up and down all these stairs at our hotel in Madrid."

I still wasn't buying it.

We sat there staring at each other in the growing darkness. I became aware again of the passing traffic down on the street. The whole purpose of my visit hung in the air. I shook my head and looked out the window.

"I'm sorry," Eva said with a touch of my hand. "But I told you to wait."

"Yeah."

"Well? You're so impulsive."

"Yeah, so you've told me."

"Well, you're here now so let's just have a good time before I have to fly home."

"Eva, what about your Uncle Augusto in Turin? I was thinking to go see him. You know, ask if he'd help us get started."

Eva shook her head as if I had uttered a blasphemy.

"Paul? You can't be serious. I'm starting college at Duke in the fall. I'm not going to abandon all my dreams just because you came to Paris."

"But I came to take care of you."

"And I told you not to."

"Great. I wish you had never sent me that goddamned telegram."

I got up and stared out the window. Eva came over and put her arms around me from behind.

"I love you, Paul, and you were very brave and gallant to come all this way but I'm not pregnant anymore."

I continued staring out at the streets of Paris, wondering if she ever had been. Either she was lying now, or she had been lying in her telegram.

But why?

Whatever it was, her story lacked the ring of authenticity.

"Come," she said and turned me around.

She kissed me sweetly and pulled me over to the bed in the growing shadows.

"Come. Make love to me in Paris."

I finally gave in to her affections. The sounds of Paris went on as we made love in the fading light, as did my doubts and suspicions.

Afterwards, we lay alone for a long time with Eva running her hand up and down my chest. I had no words to say, not ones I was prepared to speak. I could see a way for us to be happy together but what appeared to be an unspoken deception kept haunting my thoughts.

"Why can't you just come with me to Turin for a few days?" I said. "Let's see what your uncle has to say."

"Paul. You have to let it go. I'm not pregnant and I'm not abandoning all my plans on some whim of yours."

I looked away. She pulled my face back around.

"Awwwww," she said and kissed me tenderly. "You *were* awfully sweet to come all this way."

"Yeah, real sweet."

"Come on. I love you. Let's go see Paris, okay?"

I was unmoved by her continued kisses.

Some minutes later, there was a knock on the door.

"Eva?" a voice said.

"Shit, it's one of the nuns," she whispered. "Come. Get your stuff and hide in the bathroom."

"I'll be right there!" she called out to the nun.

In a mad scramble, Eva shoved the backpack under the bed. I grabbed my clothes and disappeared into the bathroom. Eva closed the door and opened the front one. She and the nun said hello.

"Are you all right?" the nun said.

"Oh, sure. I was in the bathroom." I heard Eva laugh. "You wouldn't want to go in there right now."

"Yes, I definitely smell something."

From the sound of their voices, the nun had moved part way into the room. I imagined her stealing glances at the door. There was talk of their itinerary for the next day but the whole thing sounded like a cover for checking up on Eva.

The conversation dragged on and on. Then I heard them saying goodbye and the door closing. I was dressed and sitting on the toilet when Eva reopened the bathroom door.

"You think she suspected?" I said.

"I don't know. Probably not. If she had, she would have looked in here."

"So what now?"

"You want to take a shower?"

"Yeah. I haven't had one since yesterday morning. I'm sure you can tell."

"I wasn't going to say anything."

"Thanks."

Eva came over and sat on my lap, facing me.

"I'm glad you're here."

"Why won't you run away with me? Your uncle will take care of us."

"Stop, Paul. I don't want to talk about it anymore."

"Why not? Think of the life we could make together here in Europe. It would be so cool. Why would you want to go back to that bullshit in the States?"

She pushed away and stood up.

"It's not going to happen so please stop talking about it."

"But I'm here."

She shook her head, pecked me on the cheek and started to leave.

"Hurry up and take a shower. We only have until midnight and I'm sure everyone else is dying to go out."

She left. I ran the water, undressed and showered, my frustrations ongoing. I couldn't help but think that this whole pregnancy business was bullshit.

Drying off, I heard voices and realized the other women had returned to the room. All four faces turned my way when I came out. I was wearing a blue striped jersey, jeans and my boots.

"You look like a sailor," Tanya said.

Beth and Leslie were staring at me. Eva came over and kissed me as if to mark her territory. I put the rest of my things away in my pack.

"I'm ready," I said.

"We'd better hide this back under the bed," Eva said.

With the pack tucked away, everyone moved towards the door. Eva cracked it open, poked her head out and looked both ways.

"It's clear," she said to me. "You go down first. Turn right on the sidewalk and walk up far enough so that the nuns can't see you from any of the windows."

Eva kissed me, peeked out into the hallway another time and opened the door the rest of the way. As I walked down towards the elevator, I heard the door close behind me.

Four

Downstairs, the concierge glanced up from his paperwork with a courteous nod as I passed by. The doorman opened the glass front door and also gave me a courteous nod. I thanked him and turned right with an evening breeze stirring around me. The cafés were filling up along the sidewalk. The magic of Paris was alive under the stars.

On the next block, I heard three young men conversing in English and stopped at their sidewalk table.

"Sorry. I heard you speaking English."

"Hey, a fellow yank," one of them said and held out his hand. "Chris."

"Paul."

"Have a seat," Chris said, pulling out a chair.

Chris' dishwater blonde hair was tied back in a ponytail. The other two men introduced themselves.

"Donny."

"Les."

Les had coarse dark hair and a few days growth on his chin. Donny had shoulder length, light brown hair and blue eyes. We shook hands as I sat down.

Les had already poured me a glass of wine. I took it with a glance back in the direction of the hotel. The near corner of it was still visible and it looked as if one of the nuns was staring out a window at me.

I backed out of view and explained the situation. The three of them had a good laugh.

"The truth is, they're not very catholic," Donny said.

"It's a bad habit," Les said to more laughter.

I downed the glass of wine.

"Sorry to hit and run, gents, but I really can't stick around. Hopefully I'll see you again."

"Sure. Check the Left Bank. Poke around where Montparnasse meets Saint-Michel. You'll usually find us in a café nearby. Or here. Les is big on cycling so we're at the Vendome almost every day and dig stopping at this little place on our way home."

"Cool. I'll look for you."

I got up and continued up the street. Halfway up the next block, I looked back in the direction of the hotel, saw that it was now completely out of sight and settled in against a lamppost to wait.

While standing there, a young boy came up the street carrying an empty wine bottle. The bottle was almost as big as he was. He passed through an opened door and into the dimly lit interior of an adjacent wine shop. A minute later, the boy came out cradling the now filled and corked bottle like a baby.

I watched him disappear down the street and decided to go in and explore the darkened wine shop for myself. The merchant stood behind a counter, reading Le Monde and smoking a Gauloises. A dozen or so oak barrels were stacked up on their sides behind him. On the adjacent wall, a handful of bota bags hung from wooden pegs. He greeted me in French and asked what I wanted. I pointed at the bota bags and asked how much. They were five francs. It was two francs to fill one.

I nodded and pointed at the bota bag I liked. He pulled it down from the wall and drew a sample of wine into a water glass before filling the bag. I tasted it. The wine was a musky Bordeaux, pregnant with the scent of the earth. For two francs it was good enough so I nodded again and he filled the bota bag.

While I was paying, I heard voices and looked back to see Eva and the other three women pass by the opened doorway. I took my change and hurried out to the sidewalk, the bota bag now strapped over my shoulder with the satchel.

"Hey!" I called out.

The women stopped in unison and waited for me to catch up.

"Wow, cool," Tanya said of my bota bag. "We saw those everywhere in Spain."

"Yeah, I needed something to brush my teeth with in the morning."

They laughed. We were in front of a news kiosk that also sold cigarettes. Liking the scent of the wine merchant's Gauloises, I bought a pack. It came with a small box of wooden matches. The dark scent of the cigarettes exploded into the air as I tore off the packaging. I lit one.

"Ewww," Leslie said at smelling the smoke.

I inhaled deeply and exhaled.

"They're good."

"They stink."

"Yeah. So where are we going?"

"Rue St. Michel," Eva said. "On the Left Bank to have dinner. And then on to Montmartre."

Beth and Leslie started back in with their Montmartre routine as we headed down the sidewalk.

Halfway up the next block, we came to the metro entrance and rushed down the steps under the iron and smoked glass awning. Being in a reasonably affluent neighborhood, the walls of the platform were all nicely tiled and gleaming. A few minutes later, we jumped off the subway at the Place Saint-Michel station to graffiti covered walls and a group of young musicians huddled together playing some kind of folksy, world music.

We left them a tip and went running up the stairs to the narrow street above. It was lined with three-story buildings and ground level shops. We wandered over to Rue Danton and down towards the Seine and came to Quai de Grands Augustins. From there we could see Notre Dame lit up like a stadium in the night.

"Paree!" Beth said and went running down along the river bank with her arms held out.

Her laughter echoed off into the darkness.

"Come on, stupid!" Tanya called out. "We're all hungry."

Beth turned back with her arms still held out.

"Paree! Paree! Paree!"

She ran past us and down along the river the other way.

"You're crazy!" Leslie called after her.

"She's crazy?" Tanya said. "You're both crazy. Let's go eat!"

Once Beth had returned, we started away from the river and came quickly to Place St. Michel. The plaza was lined with sidewalk cafés, shrouded by chestnut trees.

"This looks cool," Eva said of the second café we passed.

We sat down at a table close to the street. It was a pleasant summer evening with the leaves rustling overhead. All of us were in a fine mood.

"Oh stop it," Eva said when Beth and Leslie started in on their Montmartre thing again.

They said "Montmartrrrrre" several more times as if to irritate her.

The waiter came and we ordered a bottle of wine.

"Would you take a picture of us?" I asked in French and pulled the camera out of my satchel.

The five of us squeezed together and smiled.

"This is so groovy," Leslie said once the waiter had left. "I mean, being able to order a bottle of wine without getting carded."

"Yeah. I love Paris! Paree, Paree, Paree!"

"Montmarrrrrtre, Montmarrrrrtre, Montmarrrrrtre!" Leslie said and started coughing.

"Good. I hope you choke to death," Eva said.

Beth snorted and Eva snorted to make fun of her. The waiter returned with the bottle of wine and got out his pad to take our orders.

"Don't worry. I'll pay for yours," Eva whispered and squeezed my hand under the table.

The waiter ran off with our orders and Beth held up her glass of wine.

"To Paree!" she said.

"To Montmarrrrrtre!" Leslie said.

"To being young and out in the world," I said.

"Here, here," Tanya said. "I think it's so cool that you came."

We toasted and sipped our wine. The stars danced high above the chestnut trees. I looked into Eva's eyes, quietly troubled by the secret that no one would speak.

"So, tell me about your trip," I said to everyone in general. "How *was* Madrid?"

The four young women exchanged furtive glances.

"Why don't you tell us more about your trip," Beth said.

"I already did."

"Not really. You only told us about getting here from Luxembourg. How was your flight over and everything else?"

Our meals came and I explained while we ate.

"Of course, with Steve and his check business, Lufthansa was all I could afford...Actually, when I drove up to LA to apply for my passport, I stopped down at the harbor in San Pedro to see about working my way over on a ship."

"So you were going to be a merchant marine," Beth said.

"I was, until I found out how long it would take."

I explained about the British sailors.

"We'll hide you among the potatoes, mate," I said, imitating them.

"God, that would have been a trip," Leslie said.

"Yeah, only I'd have gotten here about a week too late, and that's if the captain didn't find me first."

"So what could they do to you at that point?" Tanya said.

"Throw me off at the next port, I guess. Anyway, I'm here now."

"With no way back," Beth said.

There were more furtive glances and Tanya was about to say something when Eva spoke up.

"So, are we off to Montmartre?"

"Yes, let's go," Beth said.

There was a rush to finish up and pay the bill. I wandered off a few paces while Eva took care of my share. Leslie glanced at me once and looked away. Just what the hell were these women hiding?

The tension followed us down towards the river. On our way, we heard the sound of a sax echo up from that direction, playing cool jazz.

"Wow, sounds groovy," Leslie said.

"He sounds broken hearted," Beth said.

I nodded. The music reminded me of my situation. Eva was here for two more days before heading back to the States. Then I would be in Europe all alone. The sweet and mournful melody pulled at my emotions.

At the river, we walked halfway out a bridge and turned to face the breeze. The brilliantly lit Norte Dame was behind us. The sax player was somewhere down river the other way, hidden under a quay. The sound of jazz echoed all through the warm night.

"Paree," Beth said.

"Paree," Leslie said.

I looked at Tanya. She had fixated on a handsome young man coming across the bridge.

"Bon soir," she said to him, looking hopeful.

His gaze quickly moved past her to the beautiful Beth and Leslie. Beth noticed Tanya's dejected look.

"Oh boy. Here we go. On another big *John* bummer."

"Shut up," Tanya said. "Let's just go."

"Yeah, I want to see Monmarrrrrrtre," Leslie said.

"Monmarrrrrtre, Monmarrrrrtre," Beth said.

They went running down the street beneath the chestnut trees with the three of us following along behind them.

Beth and Leslie had already descended into the metro when we arrived. We found them listening to the same group of musicians gathered against the graffiti covered wall.

When a train arrived, they ran onto it screaming, "Monmarrrrrtre! Monmarrrrrtre!"

"Idiots," Eva said with a shake of her head.

After a jostling ride across town, we ascended into a completely new set of sights and sounds. Beth and Leslie ran down the street screaming their mantra.

"Idiots," Eva said again. She turned to me. "Where shall we start?"

"How about some of Hemingway's old haunts?"

"And those would be?"

"La Coupole. Le Rotonde. Closerie des Lilas. The Dingo Bar. Les Deux Magots"

"And how do you know about these places?"

"From reading, of course."

"Reading what?"

"*A Moveable Feast*, for one."

Beth and Leslie came running back.

"Come on. What are you guys waiting for?"

"Paul wants to go see some of Hemingway's old haunts."

"Who cares about that stuffy old bullfighter?" Beth said.

I chuckled.

"Indeed."

We started down the street. Tanya and Eva got out their map and quickly located Le Coupole.

"It's the closest one," Eva said. "And then the rest of them are all right near there. Except for Les Deux Magots. It's way up at the other end of the Luxembourg Gardens."

"Maybe on our way back?" I said.

"Maybe," Beth said. "Let's just go see the first one and then we can go do something fun."

After walking two blocks, we were looking in through the windows of Le Coupole.

"See," Beth said. "A stuffy old bullfighter and his stuffy old haunts."

I had to admit. It looked pretty stuffy.

"So, can we go have some fun now?"

"We're that close to the other ones," I said.

"Oh boy," Beth said.

"They're right up the street," Eva said. "It's not going to hurt to go look."

Half a block up Rue de Montparnasse and across the street, we came to Le Rotonde, with its red chairs and red awnings. As the name suggested, it was on a rounded corner with an outdoor terrace bustling with people.

"I don't know. Looks pretty stuffy to me," I said.

Beth gave me a shove.

"Okay, let's go have a drink for good old Hemingway," she said.

We dashed across the boulevard and found a table but with only four chairs so Eva sat on my lap. The women ordered various drinks. I ordered a sherry. Beth and Leslie repeated "Montmarrrrrrtre" and "Paree" numerous times. Tanya had her eyes on every handsome young man that went by. I sat quietly with Eva's perfumed hair against my cheek, doing my best to enjoy the magic of Paris.

"Shall we have another?" I said when our drinks were nearly done.

"I want to go see the Luxembourg Gardens," Beth said.

"I don't know. Sounds pretty stuffy."

She kicked me under the table.

"I want to see them too," Leslie said.

"Fine," I said. "But isn't the Dingo Bar right around corner?"

Eva and Tanya were quickly looking at their map.

"Just across the street and down Rue Delambre half a block."

"So let's go there first and then we can maybe see Les Deux Magots on our way back to the hotel."

"Yes, because that's where Hemingway used to drink," Beth said.

"And Fitzgerald and Ezra Pound and Joyce and William Carlos Williams and…"

"All right, all right," Beth said. "Let's go see."

Eva again paid my part of the tab and we hurried on towards Rue Delambre. We found the nondescript looking bar down the nondescript looking street and peeked in through the doors.

"Stuffy," Beth said.

It was oddly elegant looking for all its plainness, with the waiters and bartenders all wearing white coats.

"Maybe the Closerie des Lilas?" I said.

"Give it up," Beth said.

Tanya glanced at the map again.

"It's right at the entrance to the gardens," she said.

"Fine. Let's go see," Beth said

She went dancing down the street singing "Paree! Paree! Paree!" and Leslie ran off with her and we did not rejoin them again until all of us had stopped at the outskirts of the Closerie des Lilas' bustling sidewalk café. It was actually more like a courtyard with the tables gathered beneath the chestnut trees.

"Cool," Tanya said.

"For being so stuffy," I said.

"Shut up," Beth said. "Anyway, let's go see the gardens and we'll come back here to party tomorrow night."

"I thought we were going to see the Eiffel Tower tomorrow night."

"Well, like that's going to take all night."

"Oh shut up," I said, mimicking her.

We went on past the café and up Avenue de l'Observatoire and were soon lost in the expansive gardens and towering hedges. Les Deux Magots was very near the far end of the gardens and we had a nightcap there before heading back towards the Seine on foot.

So consumed with our adventure, everyone had forgotten the time until Eva noticed a street clock.

"Oh god! It's quarter to midnight! We only have fifteen minutes to get back!"

As one, the four women screamed and started running up the street. I followed along behind, laughing.

At the first metro entrance, they dashed down but were already rushing back up to street level by the time I got there.

"What's the matter?" I said.

"The last subway already left," Eva said.

"So, let's just find a taxi."

"Oh, yeah! Let's just find a taxi!" Beth said.

I joined them now in a mad dash, our footsteps echoing down mostly empty streets. A taxi could not be found on the left bank so we crossed the Seine on Pont du Carousel and ran full speed across a sprawling cobblestone plaza.

"Hey, this is where they used to lop off all the heads!" I called out.

"It will be off with ours if we don't get back in time!" Leslie said.

On Rue de Rivoli, we finally spotted a cab.

"Hurry up!" Eva said to me, climbing in.

Eva had already told the driver Hotel Américain and off we went. Miraculously, we made it back with a minute to spare.

Eva kissed me while the other three women dashed inside.

"Wait here."

She was gone inside for thirty seconds before slipping back out.

"Go around back to the service entrance. I arranged for one of the bellboys to sneak you in."

47

She kissed me again.

"Hurry."

I walked down the block to an alleyway and circled around to the back of the hotel. I had been standing there for several minutes when a bellboy opened the door. He looked this way and that and waved me inside, then took me up to the fifth floor in the service elevator.

Tanya was Eva's roommate but she had snuck down the hallway with Leslie and Beth. Alone with Eva, I pleaded with her again to join me at her uncle's place, but Eva assured me that nothing of the sort was going to happen. What was the point? She was no longer pregnant.

The subject had never been raised overtly but I figured that her inheritance was the real issue at hand. Eva was not going to abandon a fortune for anyone, including me.

Her final advice was to go back to the states. We had all summer to play before she went off to college.

And then what?

It did not take a genius to read between the lines. That would be the end of it. Once she went off to college, I would never see her again.

As if nothing had happened, Eva pulled me close and made love to me again. Afterwards, we lay there in silence. There were no more reassurances now, just emptiness, and the ending up ahead.

Later, while Eva slept, I considered my next move. The world lay before me, but I would soon be broke and with an ocean between me and my journey back home. What the hell was I going to do?

I finally fell asleep but was awakened later by a knock on the door. Impulsively, I jumped to my feet and started gathering my clothes but Eva held out a hand to me.

"It's okay," she said groggily. She looked at her watch on the nightstand. "It's just the bellboy. I told him to come get you at five."

"You're sure?"

She nodded. I started to dress.

"I'll see you again tonight," she said, rubbing my back. "You know I have to be with the tour all day."

"Where are you going?"

"I don't know, but you can't be there."

"What about my pack?"

"Just leave it. Unless you need something."

"No, I'm good with my satchel. What time tonight?"

"Let's meet at the same spot. At seven?"

"All right."

The knock came again.

"You'd better go."

I felt Eva's warm, naked body beneath the sheets and wanted to make love to her again. I wanted to be in a world where nothing stood between us. Instead, I had to steal off in the night.

I kissed Eva a final time and opened the door. The bellboy was waiting and led me back downstairs. It was too early for the cafés to be open so I walked down the street to the Gare St. Lazare and tried to make myself comfortable on the rows of plastic seats. I was not alone in trying to sleep there.

When it grew light, I freshened up in the bathroom and headed for the Champs-Élysées. The first café I came across was at the end of a block with its door kitty corner to the street. Inside, two bars faced opposing windows and people stood at both of them with their espressos and café au laits, reading the papers or watching the world rush by. The morning air was rich with the usual scent of diesel fumes and baked bread.

I had a café au lait and two buttery croissants and continued on my way. The Bank of America was just off the Champs-Élysées, down a narrow side street and across from the Western Union office. All the nearby cafés were overflowing with young people waiting around for one of the two institution to open. I picked a spot against a building, out of the morning sun, and settled in to wait with the others. Each time the nearby light changed, a wave of motor scooters swooped down the block and around a corner and out of sight.

When the bank finally opened, I went in and showed a teller my check. She showed it to her supervisor. It was met with frowns.

My French being what it was, I soon had the personal attention of the bank manager. He was an elegant looking man in his forties with thick, perfumed hair combed straight back.

I explained the haste with which I had to depart and that the check was from a personal friend. He smiled sympathetically at me, turned the check over and back in his hand and shrugged.

"Ah, bon."

That I spoke French proficiently alone appeared to be enough to gain his respect and warrant his discretion and the check was cashed.

I killed part of the morning at the Louvre then went down to the quays along the Seine and smoked Gauloises and watched the old men fish and thought of Paris in the twenties. In the afternoon, I made my way over to the Jardin de Tuileries and slept on a bench until a little before six o'clock. It was lovely there in the park but I awakened in the approaching dusk with feelings of fear and melancholy.

What was I going to do once Eva left? That question dogged me all the way back to the hotel.

As I drew near, I spotted Chris and Les at the same café, seated over a bottle of wine. Chris spotted me first coming down the sidewalk and called out.

"Hey, Paul! Come join us for a glass of vino!"

Five

Chris was pouring me a glass as I sat down.

"Where's Donny?" I said.

"Oh, he fell in love," Chris said.

He and Les exchanged smiles.

"Not sure about this one," Les said. "We think she might be Hemingway's whore from *The Sun Also Rises*."

"Bad teeth and all," Chris said. "But what a figure. Ooh la la."

I nodded. Men frequently had questionable motives for the women they chose. I had never considered that to be true of me, but of late, the notion seemed increasingly possible. A man blinded by love never listened until the pain had set in. And even then...

"Here's to Paris," Chris said, handing me the glass of wine.

The three of us touched glasses and drank.

"So where's your doll?" Chris said.

"She should be coming along with her friends any time now."

"You hadn't mentioned her friends," Les said.

"Yeah. She's palling around with three of them."

Les and Chris smiled.

"They act a bit stupid at times but they're actually pretty bright. And two of them very good looking." I held up my glass. "You're welcome to take a shot."

"And you bet we will," Les said.

We sat there with the rush of cars and pedestrians passing by. Day was quickly fading to twilight around us.

"So?" Chris said. "Were you able to convince your gal to run off with you?"

"I'm still working on it."

"And if not? What's your plan?"

"I don't know. I'm trying hard not to think about that. I cashed the check today so I have a little over a hundred dollars now. How far will that get me?"

"Depends on how you spend it. In the meantime, you're welcome to crash at our place. We have a little flat over on the left bank."

"Yeah?"

"Sure. We can make room for you on the couch."

"Wow, thanks. That would be groovy."

"We also have some hashish," Les said.

"Oh wow, that would be even groovier."

"Yeah, let's see if we can get your gals to join us across the river and we'll smoke a few bowls."

"They probably will. I know I'm up for it. I haven't been high since the night I drove up to the airport."

"Bummer," Chris said.

"Coming dowwwwwwwwwwwwnnnnn," Les said.

We sipped our wine and enjoyed the evening.

Then, as if the German guns had gone off near the outskirts of Paris, the subject of Vietnam came up. Chris had run out of college deferments, which explained his reason for being there. Les had flat feet, so he was never going to be called up.

The draft wouldn't be calling on me until the following year, but it would be calling. Maybe I'd go back home, save up some money and come back to live in Paris. The life of an expatriate seemed decent enough.

A few minutes later, I heard girl's voices and looked over my shoulder.

"Here they come now."

"Which one's yours?" Les said.

"The one with the blonde hair pinned up."

"Figures."

"What?" Chris said. "That strawberry blonde and the one brunette are looking pretty good to me."

I got up to kiss Eva.

"Meet my friends, Les and Chris."

They both stood up and said hello. With Chris and Les fixated on Leslie and Beth straight off, Tanya was left to play the overly eager outsider.

"Join us for a glass of wine," Chris said and pulled two chairs over from the adjacent table.

Eva looked in the direction of the hotel and back at me. You could still see one little corner of the building from the outside tables.

"The nuns might be watching," Beth said with a mock look of fright.

A minor shuffle of chairs ensued so the women could sit farthest from the street. Chris stole some glasses from the empty table and Les poured out the rest of the wine.

"Shall we get another bottle then?"

"No, this is good," Eva said with a look at her friends. "We're off to see the Eiffel Tower in a minute."

"Why don't you come by our place and smoke a bowl of hash first," Les said.

"Wow, I'd love that!" Tanya said. "It's been over two weeks since we got high…What?" she said, looking at the other three women.

"Yeah, that would be groovy," Leslie said.

"You wouldn't take advantage of us now, would you?" Beth said.

"Never," Les said.

Beth gave him a sly look.

"That's not what I wanted to hear."

"God, Beth," Eva said with a look at the heavens.

"Well, we're game, right girls?"

Leslie smiled. Tanya was staring at Les as if in a trance.

"Okay, well I guess we might as well skip the Eiffel Tower," Eva said.

"No, no," Chris said. "It's just a lot trippier after a bowl of hash."

There was laughter as everyone polished off their wine, stood up and headed towards the metro entrance in animated conversation.

Half an hour later, we were sitting around Chris and Les' flat getting high. Their place was in Montmartre and Leslie and Beth were doing their Montmartre shtick again. The Eiffel

Tower was visible as a little miniature off in the distance, far beyond the cascade of rooftops. With the hashish, everything had taken on a dream like quality, including the tower.

"We could just sit here and pretend we went," I said.

"I'm already there," Leslie said.

"Yeah," Tanya said. "Thank you, guys. Wow, this is so cool, getting high in Paris."

Les bumped fists with Tanya but his eyes were on Beth. Chris was already lost in a conversation with Leslie.

"So, are we still going to the Eiffel Tower or not?" Eva said.

"Screw the Eiffel Tower," Beth said. "Let's go hit a café and listen to some cool music."

"I know a little jazz club," Les said.

"Okay. I'm all yours."

Seeing them click, Tanya made a desperate attempt to interject herself into Chris' conversation with Leslie. Both of them smiled her way briefly and grew lost in each other again.

"Well, shall we be off then," I said, hoping to diffuse the tension.

Getting up on our feet, we were soon stumbling back out onto the street level, laughing and talking away as a group.

Later, once we had settled in at the club, the couplings reestablished themselves, leaving Tanya as the odd one out again. When we moved to another club later on, the other two couples disappeared, leaving Eva and I alone with Tanya. Tanya was downing drinks like there was no tomorrow. You could see her getting more and more pissed at the world.

"All men are bastards," she said, looking at me.

"I know. And I came all the way to Paris to prove it."

Tanya looked at Eva and back at me.

"If only you knew."

Eva kicked her under the table. I noticed it and looked back at Tanya.

"Knew what?"

"What a sap you are."

"Shut up," Eva said. "You're just being a bitch because nobody wants you."

"Fuck you," Tanya said. "You're the spoiled brat."

"Come on, you two. It's Paris. We're supposed to be having fun."

"Yeah, some fun," Tanya said. "Someday you'll know the whole truth and then you'll laugh…And stop kicking me!" she said angrily at Eva.

"All right, let's go," Eva said. "Before I throw a drink in your face."

Eva stormed off. I stayed behind with Tanya, pissed that she had ruined our evening but dying to know what the hell she was hiding.

"So, spill it," I said. "What's this all about?"

She looked at me with glazed eyes, having grown too soused to make sense. I gave up trying and hurried to catch up with Eva.

"So what was she talking about?"

"Please, Paul. Don't start. She's just drunk and being a bitch."

"Yeah, but she was trying to tell me something. What?"

Eva stopped and put a hand to my face sweetly.

"She's just trying to ruin things, Paul. When she can't have her way, she turns into the bitch from hell."

Eva kissed me and started forward.

"Come on," she said with a hand held back in my direction.

I caught up again and took her hand.

"So where are we headed?

"Back to the hotel. I'm worn out from the whole day. I just hope Leslie and Beth know enough to get back on time."

Eva looked over her shoulder. Tanya was straggling along behind us now.

"God, she's so pathetic. I don't even want to be sharing a room with her right now."

We stopped to wait for Tanya and caught a taxi together. Tanya threw up out the window on the way back and the taxi driver went off the rails in French.

We arrived back at the hotel at a little past eleven. Eva had the bellboy sneak me up the back way as before. When I walked into the room, Tanya was locked in the bathroom. Every thirty seconds or so, we heard her retching.

A few minutes before midnight, Beth and Leslie tapped lightly on the door and came in looking as chirpy as canaries. Eva explained the situation and they somehow got Tanya down the hall to their room.

Once she was gone, Eva fell on the bed with a big sigh and stared up at the ceiling. I grabbed a clean water glass from the bathroom and filled it with wine from my bota bag. Eva shook her head when I offered it to her.

"Well I need a drink."

Eva watched me take a long slug.

"All right, give me one."

She had a long sip, set the glass down on the nightstand and held out a hand to me.

"Come."

I lay down at her side, suddenly aware again of being in Paris. The entire journey flashed through me like a jolt of adrenalin, the joys, the excitement, the uncertainties, and the secret that no one would reveal.

"I don't want you to go," I said.

Eva touched my face tenderly.

"Oh Paul. I wish I could do as you ask but I can't. You have to be practical in this world."

I smirked.

"It's true. And you've never been very good at that, have you?"

"Thanks."

"Oh, I mean it in the sweetest of ways. Honestly, Paul. You're so romantic but two people can't build a future on dreams alone. You have to get a career and work for things. It takes time and vision and a lot of hard work."

"If you came with me to your uncle's place, you'd see how hard I'd work."

"Please stop."

I started to speak again but Eva put a finger to my lips.

"Come. Just make love to me, okay? Please?"

She reached down and touched my manhood and my protests melted reluctantly into passions.

Afterwards, we lay there looking into each other's eyes.

"Let's just do something alone tomorrow night," I said.

"Okay," she said.

It was Eva's last night in Paris and my last opportunity to convince her and I wanted her full attention.

We had started to kiss again when someone knocked loudly on the door.

"Who's there?" Eva said.

A nun announced herself, and was none too happy, from the sounds of it.

Eva helped to gather my things and closed the bathroom behind me. While I hurried to get dressed, I heard the door open and a nun demand that Eva open the bathroom door. I had all my clothes back on by then but stood face to face with two nuns and the concierge.

"I want him removed immediately," the head nun said to the concierge.

He motioned for me to join him outside. I pulled my backpack out from under the bed, slung it over my shoulder, along with my satchel and bota bag and followed the concierge out the door, all under the watchful glare of two nuns. As we started down the hallway, I heard one of them telling Eva that her parents would have to be notified.

On our way down to the street, my only thought was how to rescue Eva. A thousand wild ideas flashed through my head.

At the front door, the concierge held it open and waved in a way that said, I regret the situation, monsieur, but please don't come back.

I headed down to the sidewalk café where I had met Chris and Les and Donny, not expecting to find them around at that hour but having no other plan. The place was mostly deserted. I dropped my backpack, ordered a glass of wine and sat there smoking Gauloises, wondering what to do next. It was a long way over to the left bank.

When the waiters started stacking up tables around me, I quickly finished my wine, left a tip, grabbed my things and headed for the metro. On the left bank, I got lost several times but finally made my way back to Chris and Les' place, only to find them gone. I knocked several times and went back down to the street level, suddenly struck by what I had done to myself. In Paris, completely alone and with no way home.

After walking some distance, I decided to try Les Deux Magots and was overjoyed to find Chris and Les sitting at a table outside.

"Hey, look who's here," Chris said, seeing me walk up. "Sit and have some wine, my friend."

I dropped my backpack and took a seat. Les was already pouring a glass full.

"What the hell happened?" Chris said. "You look like a man facing a firing squad."

I thanked Les for the wine, drank and explained the situation.

"Wow, bummer," Chris said when I was done. "So you think there's any chance you'll see her again?"

"I don't know. Probably not. Not here anyway. Not with all those nuns hovering around."

"They probably have a chastity belt on her right by now," Les said.

We all laughed, but the laughter quickly faded.

"Sorry, man," Chris said. "What a bummer. Fucking nuns…Well look, we'll finish up here and go smoke a bowl of hash back at our place. That should put things in a better light."

"Yeah, thanks. I could definitely use it."

Chris leaned over and patted me on the shoulder.

"It's love, man. People have been writing about this shit for five thousand years."

"I know. I know."

Chris poured the rest of the wine into my glass and ordered another bottle. Around two in the morning, the waiters started stacking chairs around us. I was feeling no pain. The waiters opened one more bottle of wine for a night cap and sat there with us for a spell before we went our separate ways.

Back at Chris and Les' place, we smoked several bowls of hash and moved on to sipping cognac. Dawn was already blushing on the horizon.

"Love and war," Chris said. "Do you realize that if it weren't for those two things, none of us would even be here right now?"

"What else is there?" I said.

"Yeah, well…"

"Here's to love and war," Les said and held up his glass.

"What the hell are you talking about?" Chris said. "You and your fucking flat feet. You probably had surgery done."

"And if it weren't for the war, I wouldn't have had to do it."

They had a good laugh at their joke.

"Ah well," Chris said to me. "Someday the war will be over and we'll *all* look back and laugh."

"In the meantime, this ain't such a bad place to ride things out," Les said.

We were soon out of things to say and got some sleep.

Later that morning, I joined Chris and Les down at a nearby café for espressos and croissants. They read the papers. I grew restless.

"Screw it," I said, standing up. "I'm going back to see what I can find out."

Both men looked up at me.

"You know where to find us."

"Thanks, Chris."

"We'll be in the usual haunts. If you get lost, come back and let yourself in. The door's never locked."

I thanked him again and started down the street. On the next block, something told me to grab my things so I stopped back at their place.

I had been loitering across the street from Eva's hotel window for a few minutes when she appeared. We both waved and stared. Then Eva motioned towards the rear service entrance. I waved back and hurried around to the alley. I had been standing there in back for quite a while before Eva finally opened the door. We hugged and kissed.

"We have to hurry," she said, pulling away. "I don't have much time."

"What happened?"

"Nothing, really. They called my parents and I'm on probation. I mean here. That's why I'm not with the tour. Tanya and another girl were sick so they left one of the young nuns to watch over us. And she's checking on our rooms every hour. That's why I have to get back."

"Please come with me," I said.

"Oh Paul. I can't. You know. My parents would disown me."

"Yeah, it's all about the money."

"Well, you try living without it."

I shrugged. I didn't have to try. I was.

"Look, why don't you go home. I checked with the consulate and they'll repatriate you if you don't have the money for a ticket. We'll have the whole summer together before I go off to college."

"Yeah. Like I could really enjoy it, knowing that would be the end of us."

"Well, maybe not. Maybe if you enrolled in college and found some direction, my parents would quit being such jerks about it."

My ears burned at hearing those words. It was a reminder of my total lack of direction. And yet my heart leapt at the offer of hope. Maybe if I went back to school, it would all work out.

Eva brushed at my tears and kissed me sweetly.

"Aw, Paul," she said. "Just go home and I'll see you there. You know I love you."

"Yeah. I love you too...But..."

Eva sighed.

"Paul. I can't stand here talking all day. I have to go."

She kissed me again.

"Good luck. And be safe."

I stared. She closed the door and I turned to leave. A few paces up the alley, I heard the door open and looked back. Eva smiled wistfully.

"What?" I said.

"I'll always remember that you came to rescue me."

She smiled sadly again and closed the door. I headed back up the alley, battling tears. I hated life then. I especially hated Eva's parents. It was medieval, your marriage arranged for you.

Out on the street, there was a thought to head back and find Chris and Les but I was too filled with grief to face anyone. I had no idea where I was going. I just knew that I had to keep moving forward. I had made it this far. I was damned well determined to continue the journey, wherever it led me.

Why the hell would I go back home? To have Eva abandon me again. I'd be a fool to buy into that grief.

I walked down to the Gare St. Lazare and paused with a look back in the direction of the hotel, still hoping to see Eva one more time, still hoping for some kind of miracle.

A few seconds later, she appeared in her window. Even at a hundred yards, I could make out the look on her face. It was something of the same wistful smile.

We both stood there staring at each other, frozen in time. Then, as if she were a maiden in a tower, acknowledging her prince, she waved. I waved back and walked into the station.

Six

The vaulted terminal was filled with airy light. Passengers bustled all around me. I stood there reading the large arrival and departure board hung from a metal beam at the center, considering where to turn next. The most obvious choice was to head east over the Alps to Eva's uncle in Turin. I had little hope of surviving without more funds. Beyond that, my choices were a matter of serendipity. I could head north to Ireland and the land of my ancestors or south to Spain through Bordeaux and the Pyrenees, but I had as much reason to go in either of those directions as I had for taking a shot at the moon.

I sat down to consider things. The image of Eva waving from the window haunted my thoughts. All this way and for what? To be abandoned over an inheritance. And Tanya's unspoken words were like poison to my heart. What the hell had she been trying to tell me? Maybe that the child was somebody else's?

With that kick in the gut, I got to my feet and decided to head south. If nothing else, Spain and its Latin sun seemed like a better place to get drunk and nurse broken hearts.

Looking at my map, I thought the village of Champlan would be a good place to start hitchhiking. It was roughly ten miles south of Paris; far enough to be clear of all the commerce around the city but not too dear in terms of a fare. Plus, the Champlan train station was less than a mile walk to the nexus of three highways, leaving a number of routes open to me.

I bought a ticket for eleven francs and went to stand on the platform. Another train departed, heading east for Strasbourg and Munich. A few minutes later, my train came in from the north. People were quickly disembarking. I hurried onboard and found a window seat. The train it turned out was mostly empty.

We departed heading west across the Seine near Courbevoie, turned south at St. Cloud and cut through the Meudon Forest. Suburbs and areas of commerce came and went, then we were deep in the forest again.

We arrived to the tiny village of Bièvres, carved out of the woods. Red rose trees crisscrossed the outdoor platform. A gendarme in a navy-blue uniform and cap walked by the train, his hands slapping a baton behind his back. Our eyes met.

The adjacent village street wound past two cottages and around a bend, disappearing into the woods. I felt a powerful urge to get off and see where it led but the whistle blew and the train lurched forward. As we pulled away from the platform, I met the eyes of the gendarme again. Then the little village and the station were lost behind us in the woods.

We passed through more forest and into a bleak area of industry. The train soon stopped at an equally bleak looking station. This was Champlan.

I got off and sat on a bench, disheartened by my surroundings. Looking at the map again, there were really only two choices; east over the Alps or south over the Pyrenees and into Spain. Either way would get me to northern Italy and Turin, though, being practical, going over the Alps was a straighter shot. With dreams of flamenco dancers in red dresses and castanets haunting my thoughts, I started off towards the highway that led east, deciding to be practical.

An access road cut into the side of a hill and crossed a bridge up ahead. A stream of cars and big trucks rushed past me. The air was heavy with diesel fumes.

Having walked some distance, I found my way over to the highway blocked by a maze of industry. Overwhelmed, I sat down in the shade of a wall and hung my head. Eva was in my thoughts. So many hopes and dreams, and all of them dashed. I longed for magic, some way to undo my fate.

I had been sitting there for a spell with the world rushing past me when a young, red-haired man with a scruffy beard appeared from a side street. He was wearing a backpack too and stopped astride me.

"What do you know, mate?" he said with a British accent. "The name's David."

"Paul."

He held out his hand. I reached up and shook it.

"Heading south, are you?

"I'm not sure. What about you?"

"South to Spain and Gibraltar. Some of me friends are in on the Paris to Dakar race and we've plans to meet up there."

"Where? In Dakar?"

"No. In Gibraltar. Why don't you come along?"

I explained about Eva and my plans to go look for her rich uncle in Turin.

"If he's rich, you won't find him in Turin. Not at this time of year."

"Why not?"

"Because all that pampered lot head down to the coast for the summer. Pretty much every bastard goes down to the coast for the summer. The big cities like Turin and Milan completely empty out."

I nodded. So, one more of my hopes and dreams dashed. David seemed to sense my distress and encouraged me again.

"Come on, mate. We'll have a bit of fun. It's better than traveling alone and you can always head over to Italy through Cinque Terra. Once in Barcelona, it's right up the road."

He held out his hand and helped me up.

"Thick or thin," he said with a pat on my shoulder. "It's always good to have a friend."

I nodded.

"I guess you know where you're going."

"That I do. We'll want to be on that highway right up there."

David led us back the way I had come and up to the end of an onramp so we could flag both the highway traffic and that coming up from the street. A good spell passed before a station wagon pulled over on the highway. A man got out wearing a tank top over his hairy chest. The car was packed

69

full of kids and a wife. Half the kids got out with him. The other half gawked through the windows.

"Where are you headed?" David asked him in French.

"Chartres. For tonight."

"Perfect," David said.

The man got busy making room for us in the far back seat without saying another word. When he was done, everyone climbed back in and off we went, with David and I facing the cars tailing along behind us.

"I was wanting to see the cathedral anyway," he confided to me.

I nodded.

"You know it?" David said.

"The cathedral in Chartres?"

"The very same one."

"I remember reading about it. One of the finest remaining examples of gothic architecture and all that."

"Bloody beautiful, it is. Think of it. There were men who spent their entire lives on this earth building that place."

"Wow, yeah. I'd never thought of it in quite those terms."

"To not have gone anywhere else? To have that be the whole purpose of your existence? Hard to imagine in this day and age."

I nodded, trying not to think of Eva while David talked, and doing a lousy job of it.

David pulled out a chunk of Gouda and some French bread from his pack.

"Fancy some?"

"Sure," I said.

I drank from the bota bag while we ate and passed it to David. The art was to guzzle the wine without touching the bag to your lips but jostling down the road complicated that operation quite a bit. David and I were both wiping wine from our chins.

I felt a bit better with some food in my gut. The pointlessness of having chased Eva over to Europe gnawed at me somewhat less. It was good just to be going somewhere, and as David had said, to have a friend.

Christ, I thought. You've always wanted to be in Europe and you're here, so enjoy it.

We passed through woods and farmland and rolling countryside. At times, the road was shrouded by trees. At others, we were looking across a vista of scattered farmhouses. We saw one castle high up on a hill and passed through the villages of Saint-Arnoult-en-Yvelines and Le Gué-de-Longroi and Champseru and were soon pulling off the highway into Chartres.

The man followed a road along the outskirts of town and eventually stopped beside a river. A sad looking parade with horns and drums was just then coming down a narrow street lined with medieval buildings.

David and I thanked the family and headed down the street, away from the cacophony.

"What's that all about?" I said.

"Oh, some saint or another...What do you say to some lunch?"

"Sure, but I really need to piss first."

David pointed across the street.

"If you can't wait, there's the public toilet."

I saw a man going into a wooden enclosure and another one coming out of it. The walls of the enclosure were so constructed that you could see the lower legs of those inside it.

"Jesus, there's no modesty," I said.

"It's the French, mate. They have none."

I left my pack with David, dashed across the street and nearly gagged going inside the enclosure. There was a line of elevated wooden seats with a hole in the concrete beneath each one. In a nod to the faint of heart, two foot pedestals had been provided in front of each seat to keep your shoes above the fray. There was a sense of shit having been thrown all about the place.

I urinated in the basin afforded for that task and hurried out.

"You look pale," David said when I returned.

"Unbelievable. There wasn't a bit of toilet paper to be found, if you had been interested."

"Like the Arabs, they use their left hand."

"Great. I don't know if I can eat now."

David laughed as we started down the street. A few blocks farther on, we came upon a little sidewalk café. There were tables out front, shaded by a gathering of trees. We parked our stuff and sat down. The day was hot but a breeze had blown up from the river, offering a bit of respite in the shade.

I ordered a Jambon-fromage sandwich with a cold beer. David ordered a Pain Bagnat with slices of hardboiled egg and his own beer. Off in the distance, over the rustling leaves, we heard the ongoing horns and drum beat of the parade.

After our meal, we walked across town to the cathedral, went inside and sat in the pews while David read off all the important trivia from his book on famous French historical sites. I stared up at the incredibly high ceilings and at the stained-glass windows and dreamed of how life would have been when the cathedral was built.

Later, we walked out to a rural highway and caught a ride south towards Tours. At sunset, we came upon the medieval town of Bonneval. The road passed through an old castle wall and continued on through narrow, cobblestone streets.

Given the hour, David and I decided to stop for the night and had the driver drop us off at the far end of town. There, a café with an outdoor terrace overlooked the road going south. In the gathering twilight, we watched the headlights coming up from Tours and Poitiers and the taillights heading off in that direction.

When the proprietor appeared, we both ordered the chicken with fried potatoes and also a bottle of wine. When the proprietor brought our food out, he sat down to talk with us.

Where were we coming from? Where were we going? Yes, we were smart to go off and see the world while we were still young. Later, the things of life would consume us and there would always be one reason or another for why we could not get away.

It was a fine conversation, about everything and nothing.

At the end of it, the proprietor told us we were welcome to sleep in his barn. David and I thanked him but slept in the field next to the barn instead. A block of forest hugged the field a few hundred yards away and it was a lovely summer night filled with stars.

A bit later, a young couple who were on the road saw our fire and joined us. We had another bottle of wine from the café and talked late into the night and eventually the couple went off to sleep by themselves near the tree line.

I awakened in the morning to David making coffee over a small burner.

"Fancy some?" he said upon seeing me stir.

"Oh, I don't know. I'm still a bit groggy from all that wine." I stood up and stretched.

"The couple?"

"They headed south already."

I nodded.

"I need to go."

David produced a roll of toilet paper with a smile.

"Thanks."

"I'd say anywhere's safe except in that direction."

Getting his drift, I veered off the other way towards the woods.

"Coffee?" he said upon my return.

I groaned and grabbed the bota bag.

"I think I'll try some of this."

"Getting an early start, eh?"

"I guess. I just need something for these damned cobwebs."

I took a long drink and broke off a chunk from what was left of a baguette. David sat sipping his coffee. He was so damned proper and organized.

I got out some of the cheese to go with the bread and chased it all down with another good gulp of the wine.

"Much better," I said.

David chuckled.

"Do you have some water?" I asked him.

"I do."

He dug around in his pack and produced a plastic bottle.

"I hope you don't mind me brushing my teeth with it."

"Not at all. We'll stock up before we hit the road this morning."

I squirted some toothpaste onto my toothbrush and walked off a few paces with the water bottle in the other hand. With my teeth clean, I rolled up my stuff and sat down. It was lovely there in the field with the forest around us but the morning sun was already growing hot on my back.

"Shall we get going?" I said.

"Absolutely. We'll be off in a minute."

I waited until David had rolled up his stuff and we started across the field towards the road. We were already beyond the old castle walls and the land was open to the road looking south. Farther on, we found a small market and stocked up with wine and cheese and bread and two apples and resumed hitchhiking. In a matter of minutes, a schoolteacher driving a Peugeot just like my old one pulled over. Robert was heading south to Provence for the summer. I sat in the back with the hot wind blowing in my face from David's open window. Robert tried speaking in his broken English from time to time but mostly we conversed in French and talked of our plans and dreams and the state of the world.

Behind it all, especially in the silences, I found myself dwelling on Eva. She would have flown off to London that morning, looking forward to the start of college in the fall and all gay about her new adventures. My game plan for that day was to stay half-drunk and try not to think of all that. Each thought of her was like a knife in my heart.

Just south of Tours, Robert took the turn towards Bourges and dropped us off. A field of wheat beside us waved in the summer breeze. David stuck his thumb out. I sat down and got comfortable against my backpack. There was an urge to crawl in among the wheat and take a nap.

Once again, I was failing miserably at keeping Eva out of my mind. It would have been easier just to break down and weep but the tears would not come. Anyway, I was not about to let David or anyone see my grief.

A farmer in a stake bed truck picked us up a short while later. It was good to be moving forward again.

Here and there along the highway, I saw cars pulled to the side of the road and men standing there behind an open door, pissing into the grass. The day was very hot. When I wasn't thinking of Eva, I was thinking of cool places like alpine meadows or a day in the surf.

The farmer turned off at the little village of Beaumont and left us alongside the highway again. Farmhouses dotted the rolling countryside. David and I had been there five minutes or so when this young couple got dropped off fifty yards past us. The woman waved so we walked over to say hello.

"You are going to Spain south too?" she said in broken English.

We nodded.

"We from Czechoslovakia."

The woman patted her chest in saying this. David and I exchanged glances. Everyone hated the Russians for invading their country.

"We stop in Poitiers for the night. And you?"

I shrugged.

"Maybe for something to eat," David said, "but we'll be heading on for someplace to camp."

"You join us for something to eat first, yeah?" she said. "We have no friends to talk with in days."

"Sure, sure."

"Irenka."

"Nikola."

The introductions done, the four of us got comfortable alongside the road and Irenka stuck out her thumb. An hour went by without anyone stopping.

Just as we were thinking to split up, another young couple in a Volkswagen bus pulled over. Things were quickly rearranged in back to make us comfortable and we rode into Poitiers drinking wine and sharing a spirited conversation.

In Poitiers, Irenka and Nikola seemed to know their way around and led us to a neighborhood of shops and cafés. We chose a place with outdoor tables, ordered wine and meals and sat there taking in the cool evening breeze. It being that time of day when lovers were out strolling with lovers, my thoughts naturally turned towards Eva again.

"We hoping to find work," Irenka said.

"You wanting work?" Nikola said.

"I'm on vacation," David said.

"Are you two looking for work," I said.

"Yes. We go to Spain."

"For work?"

"Yes. Picking crops."

"Oh."

They seemed eager and hopeful and nervous all at once. When the wine came, Nikola held up his glass.

"Just for tonight we enjoy the wine, yeah?" he said.

We toasted and drank and in the course of the conversation learned that Irenka and Nikola had been students in Prague, had fought in the resistance during the Russian invasion, were forced to hide from place to place in the city and ultimately fled to the country. And when even that sanctuary had failed them, they crossed over the border into West Germany, applied for asylum and had worked the past year as migrant pickers. They were headed to Spain now for the early crops and as summer turned towards fall, would work their way back north until they were picking grapes in Bordeaux.

As refugees with asylum status, they were free to go anywhere in Europe but not particularly welcomed in doing so.

It was getting on towards nine when Nikola poured the last of three bottles and everyone began to yawn.

"Well best if we try to get beyond the outskirts of town somewhere," David said to me.

"No, no," Nikola said. "Stay with us. We find a place right here."

"I don't fancy sleeping in an alley," David said

"No, no. You follow. We find a nice place. With a view!"

Nikola had said this last with a big smile.

All of us chipped in for our share of the bill and gathered our things. Nikola led the way. As we neared the center of the city, David grew increasingly suspicious and let it be known by way of a look that this was no place he wanted to be.

Still, we followed the couple for a few more blocks and came upon another district of cafés and shops. Nikola pointed hopefully across the street at a large store. It was in a state of construction and draped with a heavy sheet of plastic across the entire front. Nikola pointed at a second story balcony and waved to us as he and Irenka hurried across the street. When we failed to follow, Nikola waved with more urgency.

"Come, come."

By the time we had crossed over, Nikola was pulling the plastic loose from one end of the storefront.

"Come," he said. "We go sleep upstairs."

"I don't know, mate," David said with a look at me. "This isn't exactly my sort of mischief."

I shrugged. Nikola smiled back at us and disappeared behind the plastic with Irenka.

"Let's go find our own way," David said.

The two of us had started off when we heard a soft whistle and looked up to find Nikola and Irenka staring down from the balcony. Nikola threw out his arms triumphantly, as if to say, how do you like my view!

With a shrug at David, I pulled back the sheet of plastic and slipped inside the storefront. Nikola was waiting for us when we came out onto the balcony.

"A wonderful view, no?" he said. "We even have private bathroom and drinking water."

I shrugged at David.

"No, you see," Nikola said. "The goddamned Soviets, they taught us something. Irenka and I, we are the very best at finding little places to hide in any city."

Nikola waved at the balcony floor as if offering it to us.

"Our home for the night! We get up early and..." Nikola wiped both hands together to finish his thought. "No one even knows we were here."

Seven

I arose once in the night to use the bathroom and drink from a water fountain before returning to my sleeping bag. The summer heat had dissipated and the city below was utterly still, save for the occasional truck rumbling by off in the distance.

I found myself picturing Eva again, snuggled up in warm sheets, the sweet life ahead of her. My own fate was more like something out of a thousand and one nights, an evil spell cast, a young man swept across the world, misfortune befalling him again and again. I turned over on my other side, eyes open, praying for sleep to overtake these thoughts.

I was awakened before dawn by the sounds of Nikola and David rolling up their gear. The sky was barely light. A fog hung over the town.

"We hurry, my friend," Nikola whispered. "The city awakening now."

I heard the voices of merchants and the sound of increasing traffic. The scent of freshly baked bread was on the morning breeze. In France, you could be completely blind and know it was dawn by that one thing.

I yawned and got up. Irenka was nowhere in sight. I needed to use the bathroom and assumed she was already in there. I had my stuff all rolled up by the time she returned and I took her place.

With everyone ready, we started downstairs together. The sky had started to blush pink in the east.

Nikola peeked out through the plastic before waving for us to join him. I was the last one out and heard a man shouting from up the sidewalk. The others were already running and I hurried to catch up with threats being hurled after us.

At the first café, we parked our gear by the door, ordered cafe au laits and croissants and sat there with our backs to the storefront, soaking up the morning sun and having a laugh over our close call. It was agreed that once we reached the highway, we should split up and try to hitchhike separately.

On the way out of the city, we stopped at a boulangerie and stocked up on bread and cheese. I also stopped to refill my bota bag at a wine merchant.

Out on the highway, Nikola insisted that David and I go first but we gave them the first shot and were several hundred yards up the road when they caught a ride. With a final wave goodbye, we watched them disappear.

"It's a trip, isn't it?" I said to David.

"What is, mate?"

"The way Europe is broken up into these little state sized countries. Something completely different could be going on politically speaking right next door. It would be like there's a civil war going on in Alabama but everything's still normal in Georgia."

"But it is sort of that way, isn't it? With the civil rights movement and all? You could be lynched in one state but not in the other."

"Yeah, I guess, but it's still different. It's all the different languages and cultures. And we don't exactly have the Russians invading us."

"No, just the British," David said with a smile.

I nodded.

"Yeah, and being Irish, I've been meaning to discuss that with you."

"Bloody heathens."

"Bloody black hearted Prods."

"I'll drink to that."

"Hey, there's an idea."

I swiveled my bota bag from around in back and had a good swig.

"Care for some?"

David shook his head.

"Do you always drink in the morning?"

"No. Only when I've been abandoned in France by my girlfriend and don't have enough money to get back home."

"Fair enough, mate. Fair enough."

I had another long swig, capped the bota bag and stuck my thumb out. To hell with Eva. She could have her privileged life. I was off to the Pyrenees and a grand adventure.

The minutes passed and I was back to thinking of Eva. I both longed for her and hated her. I especially hated not knowing the secret those four women had kept hidden from me.

David and I were very fortunate and caught a ride with a young couple going straight through to Biarritz. David planned to spend the night there, cross into Spain the next morning and catch a train over the mountains. I planned to go with him that far. Then David would be off on his Paris to Dakar adventure and I would be on my own again. Through forest and farmland, I remained dogged by these thoughts.

As we neared Bordeaux, the terrain flattened out into the Lore River delta. The couple planned to stop for lunch but did not want to fight the traffic around Bordeaux and pulled off the highway at Ambarès-et-Lagrave, well beyond the outskirts of the city. We found a café downtown, talked of life and traveling over lunch and were back on the road within the hour.

It was getting on into late afternoon when the couple pulled into Biarritz and parked in front of their hotel. The four of us said goodbye and David and I started down Avenue de la Marne towards the shore. In the late breeze, all the white buildings were brilliantly etched against the blue sea.

I had thought to bring along a bathing suit and we were soon refreshing ourselves in the surf on a hot summer day. After the swim, David and I took our things and moved over to the other side of Roche du Basta, away from all the tourists. Having made ourselves comfortable in a little cove, we watched afternoon fade to evening, then changed and walked into town and had dinner at a café with a view of the coast. The wine was cheap and the food good and we had a fine time watching the tourists come and go while talking with our fellow travelers.

David had intended to splurge for a hotel room that night but the entire town was booked up so we followed a path along the rocky coast, looking for a place to camp. The sea broke against the cliffs down below us and the warm summer evening was thick with a salty mist.

We eventually passed through a tunnel carved into the rock by the surf and came to a point. The Aquarium de Biarritz stood high on a promontory above us. It was closed for the night and the lights were all out.

"What do you say we look for a spot up there to bed down?" David said.

"Sounds good to me."

We zigzagged up towards the promontory along another rocky trail and came upon a row of outdoor salt water tanks near the front of the building. It was too dark to see inside them but I was reminded of shopping for seafood with my parents as a boy, the rows of tanks filled with Maine lobsters. I peered into the dark water more closely but was still unable to make out what was inside the tanks.

We continued around to the south end of the building and found a secluded terrace with a view of the sea. The muted sound of the surf whispered off in the distance. We shared a bit of wine and conversation before getting to sleep.

Sometime later, we were startled awake by a sharp voice.

"Debout! Debout!"

I felt a club in my back and rolled over to find two gendarmes standing over us.

"Debout! Debout!" the one closest to me said again.

David and I climbed out of our sleeping bags and were asked to produce our papers.

"Why are you sleeping here?" the one gendarme asked while reviewing them.

We explained that we had intended to rent a hotel room but could not find any vacancies. Suspicious, he asked if we had any money. We showed him what cash we possessed and that eased the tension a bit.

The two gendarmes spoke quietly among themselves before issuing their verdict. It would be all right for us to say for one night but we were to be gone with the morning light. We nodded. They nodded back and continued on their rounds, both of them slapping at their clubs behind their backs.

"Decent of them," David said as he settled back in.

"Debout! Debout!" I whispered and we both chuckled.

Unable to sleep now, I lay there looking up at the stars.

"Have you ever been to Spain?" I asked David.

"Several times."

"What's it like?"

"Well, you wouldn't want to be doing this on Spanish soil. They'd arrest you and throw you in a dungeon?"

"Really?" I said looking over.

"Well, maybe not a dungeon but they wouldn't be nearly as civil. Franco and the fascists are still in power, you know. They're still fighting an unspoken war."

"Bummer."

"Yes, but keep your nose clean and you won't have any trouble."

David was soon asleep. I lay there thinking of Franco's Spain and Eva.

In the morning, David and I went down to the sea for an early swim, then changed and stopped for cafe au laits on our way out of the city. It was only fifteen miles to the border now and we quickly caught a ride straight through.

As David had warned, the atmosphere changed dramatically at the border. The Spanish guards were brusque and suspicious and went through every bit of our belongings, then carefully examined our papers before finally waving us into Spain. We walked several blocks through the little town of Irun, bought two tickets to Pamplona at the train station and boarded the train.

Every car on the train was packed with peasants. David and I went through several cars before finding two empty seats. The windows of the train were open and everyone's belongings were spilling out into the aisles. The man across from us had a wooden cage on his lap with four nervous chickens crammed inside.

There alongside the tracks, I spotted two soldiers wearing black patent-leather, tricorn hats.

"Who are they?" I asked David.

"La Garda. It's Spain's version of the SS. These are the blokes who'll toss you into a dungeon."

"Great."

"Just don't look at them funny."

"I'll work on that."

The train pulled out of the station and started up a long, steep incline. I stole glances at the peasants around us. They were all weathered by the sun and as serious as a funeral.

The train soon came to the crest of the hill and started back down to the sea at San Sebastián. After a brief stop there, the line continued south to Andoain and turned southeast up into the mountains. At times peaks hugged the tracks around us. At others we had vistas of distant villages, far, far down the steep grassy slopes. On several occasions, as the train struggled on its way up the mountain towards Idiazabal and Altsasu, we saw more of La Garda walking alongside the tracks. They too were as serious as death, and well-armed.

The train stopped at a small station. Some peasants got off. Others got on.

At Altsasu, the line turned back north in a slow, steady ascent towards Pamplona. The mountain eventually gave way to a vast plain and half an hour later we entered the city. The snowcapped peaks of the Pyrenees stood off in the distance.

David led us to a wooded area along the Arga River and a campground a mile or so north of town. We rented a tent from the owner, promptly set it up, stored away our belongings and headed back towards town across a wide marshland. That led to a district of old homes and we had been walking along the narrow, winding streets for some time when one of them suddenly dumped us out into a large plaza. The plaza was encircled by bars and restaurants and swarming with people, the festivities spilling out onto the streets from inside various establishments and surging back inside again without any clear demarcations. On a warm, summer evening, it was one giant party, with music and laughter filling the air.

I spotted an old man with white hair and a white beard, seated at one of the outdoor tables.

"Wow. It's Hemingway come back to life," I said.

David laughed.

"Pretty good knock off, eh mate? People treat him like a god. All his drinks are free. As much as he can guzzle. You'll find several of them around town but he's definitely the best. Been a fixture at the running of the bulls ever since I've been coming."

"The running of the bulls?! Wow. Why didn't you tell me?"

"I thought you knew."

"I know it exists. I didn't know we were stumbling into it."

"Well we're definitely in the thick of it now, mate and will be for a week. The town basically shuts down for the party."

"Wow. What a trip."

"Actually, we're a day late. The mischief started up yesterday. Come on."

David led me across the plaza and past a throng of people crowded outside one of the bars.

"Not here," he said over the din. "We won't be getting served in that pub any time soon. There's a quieter place this way."

We headed down to a corner of the plaza where the festivities were modestly more subdued and had started into one of the bars when a rumba line snaked out of the bar next door. A group of musicians was leading the way with the signature rhythm. Da da da da da *da*... Da da da da da *da*...

A young woman grabbed me by the waist and dragged me into the line. Someone grabbed David and the line snaked into the next bar where we were cheered on by the patrons. On and on it went by, in and out of every bar around the plaza, with and drinks being poured down our throats and the musicians leading the way.

Half drunk and needing to piss, David and I eventually broke away from line.

"Follow me," he said. "There's a public loo at the far end of the plaza."

We walked over to where the plaza abutted a busy avenue and then down below street level along a set of tiled stairs. The spacious bathroom was tiled floor to ceiling and sparkling clean. An attendant greeted us as we walked in.

"What's with him?" I asked David while we were draining our bladders.

"They keep the place clean and pass out towels for a peseta tip."

I heard a man retching in one of the stalls behind us.

"He's got his work cut out for him back there."

David smiled and yanked up his zipper. I joined him in freshening up a bit at one of the sinks. The attendant handed us a clean towel and we each left him a peseta for his troubles.

"I'm famished," I said, back up to the streets.

"Likewise, mate, but let's move further away from the plaza. Everything around the old Hemingway lot is overpriced."

We headed down a narrow, winding backstreet in the direction of the bullfight ring and came to a quiet restaurant with a worn, wooden door. David checked the menu tacked to the wall outside and nodded.

"This seems to be in our budget."

We both ordered paella with a cold beer and felt halfway sober for having eaten.

On our way back to the plaza, we found a place to fill my bota bag and settled in at a safe distance to watch the festivities. At three in the morning we found our way back to the campground and were not ready to face the world again until eleven the following morning.

By noon we had showered and were back in the city. The run of the bulls was long over but people were milling around everywhere now, in anticipation of the afternoon bullfights. David wanted to attend so we walked over to the bullring first thing and bought two tickets.

It being very hot in the sun, we walked back in the shade of a narrow street and slipped into the cool interior of the first suitable bar we found. They had cheap empanadas so we ordered two each of those, along with cold beers, and nursed the beers until it was time to go back to the bullring.

"My older brother Joseph had a poster of Manolete," I said on our way across town.

"Yeah? The bloody best there ever was, some say."

"Yeah. I remember the poster hanging from his bedroom door. A bullfight on such and such a date in Madrid. Manolete looked very gallant with his cape and sword and all."

"Killed by a bull, you know."

"Yeah. I remember my brother telling me that."

In the heat of a listless afternoon, the idea of killing bulls seemed especially grim but when we walked into the bullring, the atmosphere was surprisingly festive. What appeared to be a queen and members of her royal train were seated directly above us, the woman's long, straight black hair adorned with a crown and black veil. When the toreros entered the ring, they all bowed in her direction and the entire stadium seemed to do so in unison. Our seats were in the sun. David and I ordered a cold beer from the first passing concessionaire.

Following a blare of horns, the first bull bolted into the ring and promptly chased everyone back over the boards. The crowd went wild and the queen waved her laced handkerchief for everyone to see.

Then the torero who had been chosen to fight this bull entered the ring along with the banderilleros and each took their turn testing the bull's rush. Next, the picador rode in on his blindfolded horse and the bull immediately rushed them, its horns digging into the heavy padding as if hoping to lift the horse off the ground. All the while, the picador was digging his lance deep into the morillo of the bull's neck.

The three banderilleros had returned to the ring by this point and took turns making passes and sinking their banderillas into the neck of the bull. If the purpose of all this was to tire the bull and lower its head, they had succeeded on both accounts.

When the torero strutted back into the ring, the crowd grew hushed. The bull was staring dumbly with its head hung low. Things were not going the way the beast had imagined.

I was not the one to say if this pageantry was proceeding as planned, but the torero looked to be doing an admirable job until he went for the kill, or estocada, and the sword hit bone instead of sinking into the bull's heart. By the time a second pass had failed, and a third one, the crowd was booing and hissing and offering catcalls. The entire stadium was at the man mercilessly. I half expected him to turn the sword on himself.

Disgraced, the torero finally came forth with a different sword and used it to prick the bull's nose. This had the effect of lowering the bull's head further, whereupon the torero took a whack at the back of the bull's neck, as if to sever its spinal cord. When this too failed to kill the bull, a dagger was employed to complete the job.

By now, the torero could not have fled Pamplona fast enough. No establishment in town existed where he would not have been shamed. The queen gave what amounted to a thumbs down. A team of mules raced into the bullring and the bull's body was unceremoniously dragged out through a set of wide, wooden doors.

Some of the ensuing performances fared better and the queen was petitioned to award one torero with the ear of a bull. Another torero was gored but finished his estocada and received a ride out of the ring on the shoulders of his compatriots and cheers for his courageousness.

David seemed to know all about these matters and commented aside to me as necessary so I would know what the hell was going on. Actually, my brother Joseph had left a copy of Hemingway's *Death In The Afternoon* lying around the house when I was a boy and I had found the introduction very wry and interesting, where Hemingway was attempting to explain the refinements of bullfighting to a fictional woman. The rest of it had seemed rather gruesome. I had never been fond of machoism and blood and the likes.

I understood that the whole experience was meant to be cathartic, like a Greek play, a cause for reflection about mankind's mortality, but with actual blood involved, I could not move on fast enough.

On our way out of the ring that day, David and I saw the last bull being slaughtered. The poor were lined up for the meat. The alley behind the ring ran red with blood.

Eight

Late that afternoon, a few streets off the main plaza, David and I stepped up to a bar and ordered drinks. It was a relatively quiet establishment for Pamplona, especially for that week. Music played quietly over subdued conversation and laughter. Flies busied themselves in the listless heat.

A cheerful looking fellow with long, straight hair and a tie dye headband stepped up to the bar next to us and ordered a drink.

"British, right?" he said, having heard David speak.

"I am. Paul here's a Yank."

"Irish, actually," I clarified. "I like to keep our differences in proper perspective."

The young man laughed and offered his hand.

"Billy."

"David. And you've already met our barefooted heathen here."

"Hey, why don't you two join us?" Billy said. He pointed at a corner table, where four young women and two men were enthralled in conversation. "We're one dude short of a perfect

95

match. Well, now we'll be one doll short of a match but what the hell. We can always find another lady."

While waiting for his drink, Billy got into a conversation with David about the Paris to Dakar race. I glanced again at the table. One of the women had blonde hair and appeared to be coupled with a blonde-haired man. The other three ladies looked to be Spanish by their long black hair. The most beautiful of the lot met my gaze for a moment and looked away. Castanets were suddenly at work in my heart.

A minute later, the bartender brought Billy's drink and we followed him over to his table. A young man with coarse dark hair and a dark beard was talking animatedly over everyone else but paused and stood up upon our arrival.

"Well, goddamn, hello," he said, shaking our hands. "Stewart's the name. And you're?"

"David."

"Paul."

"Well, there's one too many of you bastards but we'll just have to look for another Spanish beauty. Have a seat, have a seat."

In one motion, the boisterous Stewart gave us both a triumphant pat on the back, helped us to get comfortable and downed the rest of his mojito.

"This is Franz and Annah, by the way, and Conchita, Rosa, and Anastasia. Be careful with Franz here," Stewart said as if aside to me. "He's a German intellectual and they're a bloodless lot."

Franz stared at me without emotion, his broad forehead accented by cool, blue eyes and a bit of peach fuzz on his chin.

"See?" Stewart said. "The bastard could eviscerate you with that goddamned stare of his."

"You're the bastard," Franz's girlfriend Annah said with a laugh.

Annah could not have been more the opposite of Franz with her cheerful, round face and short blonde hair.

With the conversation spilling this way and that around the table, I stole another glance at the three Spanish ladies. Conchita was tall and horse faced, Rosa petite and intense, Anastasia simply enchanting. She looked my way again and stared.

To hell with you, Eva, I thought. I've just found someone who will appreciate my gallantry.

When Stewart's next mojito came, he held it up to everyone.

"Here's to goddamned Hemingway," he said and drank.

Stewart was trying very hard to play the role, and doing a reasonably good job of it.

Meanwhile, a version of *Malaguena* came on, just a guitar and vocal. I stood up and held out my hand to Anastasia. She hesitated but ultimately joined me on the floor.

"Here's to goddamned romance!" Stewart called out and saluted with his mojito.

I had to smile over Stewart and all his Hemingway bullshit but my eyes were locked on Anastasia. We were the only ones in the bar right then, and the only two people in the universe, as far as I was concerned.

When the song ended, we returned to the table and rearranged things so we could sit together. Anastasia sipped at her drink and stared at me over the glass.

"Do you speak English?" I asked.

She shook her head and tapped her thumb and index finger together.

"French?" I said. "Francoise?"

She nodded so I asked in French where she was from and how she had gotten to Pamplona and what her plans were and learned that she and her two friends had taken the train up from Madrid and planned to be there all week but had to be back at work the following Monday.

Madrid again, I thought. Well, I could always go there instead of Turin. Find a job and become a Spanish citizen. I was ready to go anywhere and do just about anything to be with Anastasia.

As if we were already in love, Anastasia learned her head against my shoulder and picked at my hand with hers. And that sweet gesture alone said more to me about love than any book I had ever read.

Lost in our own little world, I heard bits and pieces of the conversation around us and gleaned that Stewart was a student and political organizer at Columbia, Billy had a head shop up in Vermont, Franz taught philosophy at Bonn, Annah was his wife and this rather odd collections of souls had come together when Annah said hello to the Spanish ladies an hour earlier. Then Billy and Stewart had sauntered into the bar, were allured by the three Spanish beauties, as any two young men would be, and there we were.

The drinks and laughter flowed, the increasingly raucous conversation rendered partly in English, partly in Spanish but mostly in French, as no one besides Franz and Annah spoke German and French was the one common language among us.

In the course of the revelry, Stewart announced that while in Pamplona he planned to go fishing up in the Pyrenees and drink wine and fight bulls and make love to Spanish women and in general live out his own version of *The Sun Also Rises*. I had no interest whatsoever in reviving Hemingway but thought the idea of going up into the mountains was a good one, even if it was just for one day. Anything to get out of the oppressive heat.

In the wee hours of the morning, before leaving the bar, I had the waiter take a picture of us together with my camera. Out in front, a general consensus was reached that we would meet for the run of the bulls at seven, have breakfast and thereafter catch a bus up to Roncesvalles. Billy and Stewart were in the vanguard on the planning. The Spanish ladies would be our guides.

I went with Anastasia to her hotel room and did not see David again until all of us reconnected in the streets the next morning. He and Billy and Stewart had already jumped the wooden barricade and were badgering me to join them.

"I'm perfectly fine with observing the madness from right here. Photo, though?"

I got up onto the barricade and the three of them stood arm in arm for a picture, David completely decked out in white, campesino clothing, the other two having made do with a red bandanna around their necks. Stewart was wearing a heavy, latigo leather jacket in the morning heat.

"This ought to piss off a bull or two," he said about the jacket.

We were having a good laugh over that when, in a frenzy of shouts and screams, a mob of young men came running down the narrow street with the bulls hard on their heels.

"Here they come!" I shouted from the top of the barricade.

"Holy shit!" Stewart said, narrowly dodging the first one.

With one bull after another plowing through the crowd, our three compatriots were swept along and quickly lost in the chaos.

I rejoined Anastasia and the others and together we followed the swarm of humanity in the direction of the bullring. By the time we arrived, the bulls were in the actual ring and half the town had poured in after them. From the fringes of the mob, I located Stewart and guided everyone in that direction.

"Look at this! Look at this!" he said, proudly displaying a gash in his leather jacket.

Both he and Billy related their near death brush with the bulls. Meanwhile, the bulls were still in the ring, sending ripples of terror through the crowd. The men in charge of the corrida de toros eventually got the bulls funneled into their underground corrals and the crowd slowly dispersed. We agreed to find a quiet place to eat and moved with everyone else towards the exit.

Back out on the street, we started towards the main plaza, quickly found a cool, quiet café to hide from the morning heat, ordered cold beers to go with our breakfast of blood sausage and eggs and listened to more of Stewart and David and Billy's adventures. Billy had secured the tickets for our trip up into the Pyrenees and we left for the bus station shortly after finishing our meals.

When we arrived, the bus seats were already overloaded so Stewart insisted on sitting on top. With much reluctance, the ladies joined us and off we went, the feeling of being thrown to our deaths visceral each time the bus swerved around a curve.

We arrived intact at Roncesvalles an hour later. It was a clean little mountain town of white buildings and red roofs with the grassy shoulders of the low Pyrenees rising up behind it. It was my impression that any fishing to be had would involve a long hike, as it had for Hemingway in the novel, but Stewart and Billy were no less determined and somehow found a store owner to rent them some gear. Off we all went with enough cheese, bread, wine and fruit to make it a picnic.

When we came to a shallow stream at the base of the hills, Stewart and Billy waved goodbye and embarked on their way further up into the mountains. We heard them singing away until at last their voices disappeared. By then we were all lying on our backs on blankets the ladies had brought along. I had Anastasia at my side and was looking up at the blue sky, hardly remembering those dismal events back in Paris. The sweetness of Anastasia's presence had subsumed all of my former grief. I was now a Roncesvalles knight of old and Anastasia was my princess, my one and only true love, and I whispered sweet things in her ears and the cool breeze whispered in the pines above our heads and the stream gurgled by while the others talked and laughed around us. When I wasn't dreaming valiant dreams, I was dreaming of how I would make love to Anastasia again that night and if Eva crept into my thoughts at all, it was simply to remember what a foolish young woman she had been and how foolish I had been to chase after her. And of course to wonder what on earth was the dark secret she had been hiding.

The talk had turned to jokes of Stewart and Billy returning with minnows instead of trout when we heard their voices from high up on a hill, singing away. They were small white specks against the green grass but kept growing larger. Then they briefly disappeared into the hollow of the stream before reappearing empty handed, save for their poles.

"Not much luck with the fish, I see," I called out. "Any luck finding Hemingway?"

"I'll find you Hemingway," Stewart called back.

There was laughter as the men dropped their poles at our feet.

"We'll have some of that wine," Billy said.

Franz handed him the bottle and both men took a long drink to quench their thirst.

"So, nothing?" David said.

"We did see some grand looking trout," Billy said.

"The one that got away," Stewart said. "But, god, the view. You should have joined us. Higher up you can see down across this valley and all the way back to Pamplona."

"Sounds lovely," I said, "but I'm quite content with the wine in my veins and the wind in my ears."

Stewart took note of Anastasia stroking my chest.

"So I see."

"Said the blind man to the deaf and dumb."

Steward laughed.

"You are Irish."

"I am, thank god."

"So, are we heading back before nightfall?"

Everyone nodded.

"But not sitting on top of your bus," Conchita said in her heavily accented English.

She repeated it in Spanish and then in French for the benefit of Franz and Annah.

Amidst the ongoing banter, I closed my eyes and pressed Anastasia's hand hard against my chest. In that fleeting hour, the longing for Eva had somehow returned like a cancer. I saw her blonde hair and sparkling blue eyes and felt all the old feelings and did not understand how all these disparate things could exist in one heart.

With all the wine bottles empty, it was as if a bell had tolled and everyone began to stir. The late afternoon sun grew low over the mountains and we started back towards Roncesvalles singing songs to ward off the rush of darkness.

Dusk had filled the main plaza by the time we arrived back to Pamplona and we fell into the same revelry as the previous evening. Again, I went with Anastasia to her hotel room and when I returned to the camp the following morning to check on David and change my clothes, he was nowhere to be found.

Feeling exhausted from all the late-night festivities, I lay down in the tent to take a brief nap and did not awaken again until midafternoon. Unsettled by the late hour, I hurried to shower and ran back to town, having made plans to meet Anastasia and the others for lunch and worried now that I might have missed them.

When a quick check of all the bars around the plaza failed to turn up anyone, I hurried over to Anastasia's hotel room and knocked. There was no answer so I returned to the lobby and learned the three women had checked out.

How could that be? Anastasia would not have left town without telling me.

I raced back to the plaza and revisited all the bars, still with no luck. I stood there alone in the fading light, with no idea where to turn next.

Recalling all the backstreet cafés and bars and restaurants we had haunted over the past few days, I made the rounds, with no better luck. I went to the bullring and circled it several times. There was a thought to go in but it cost 75 pesetas and I was running low on funds.

With renewed panic, I quickly counted up what was left. Little more than twenty American dollars. The idea of finding Eva's uncle jumped in me again. I was alone and six thousand miles from home and had no way back.

Hungry and wanting a drink, I found a place to fill my bota bag, bought an empanada and found a shady place to sit in the plaza.

Late in the afternoon, with the crowd pouring back from the bullfights, I spotted Stewart and Billy going into a bar and hurried over to join them.

"Hey, Paul!" Billy said. "I guess you must have heard."

"No. Heard what?"

"Rosa's mother had a heart attack so the three of them took a plane back to Madrid. Anastasia was looking everywhere for you."

Stewart pulled out a piece of paper from his pocket.

"She left her address and told you to come."

I took the note and stared at it. It was signed 'con amor, Anastasia'.

"Oh man."

"Hey, brother," Billy said. "Don't be bummed. That chick really loves you."

"Yeah, but I'm nearly broke and my only hope is getting to Turin to find Eva's rich uncle."

"I say get your ass down to Madrid. You've got it made with Anastasia."

"Yeah, I guess…So where's David?"

"Oh, shit. I almost forgot. He split too."

"What? I just slept in our tent this afternoon and his shit was still there."

"Yeah, I guess he got a telegram from his friends down in Gibraltar an hour ago. Apparently they were ready to head south so he took the next train out."

"What about my backpack?"

"He said he would leave it with the owner of the campground."

"Great. I'd better head over there before I lose my stuff."

I looked around the bar with a growing sense of anxiety.

"Look, man," Stewart said. "You can crash with us tonight, no problem."

Billy had ordered three beers and offered me one.

"Cheers. Everything'll work out. The universe has a way of taking care of us."

"Yeah, I guess."

"No, trust me. Everything will be fine."

He clinked his bottle to mine and we drank. My head was churning.

"Did you want us to walk over to the campground with you?" Billy said.

"Yeah, that would be cool. Thanks."

"Sure," Stewart said. "In fact, I'll tell you what. Billy and I'll treat you to a meal and a night on the town. We'll even help you with the ticket to Madrid if you need it."

"Thanks, brother, but you don't have to do that."

"No, man. The three musketeers and all that. Let's just go get your shit and then we'll drink and be merry."

I looked off in the distance, missing Anastasia terribly and hung up with a million concerns but truly thankful for their companionship.

"Man," I said. "I'd really love to get high right now."

"Yeah," Stewart said. "That's something you really want to be careful about in this country. Right Billy?"

"Yeah. This guy we met? He told us his friend got nailed and was looking at fifteen to twenty. Can you imagine it? These fascist bastards don't fool around. They just throw your ass in a dungeon."

"I'd still like to get high. I'm just really bummed out right now, you know?"

"Hell," Stewart said. "Let's try a shot instead."

He ordered three brandies and then three more and by the time we left the bar to go gather my stuff, were feeling no pain.

That night, I drank liquor like never before, but in the morning, the emptiness remained, as did my dilemma. Go south to Madrid with hopes that everything would work out with Anastasia, or head for Turin in hopes of finding some work. As Eva had said, being practical was not my strong suit, but even I could see the impending disaster. If things did not work out in Madrid, I would be stranded there without a dime to my name. At least Turin held out the prospect of work. I could make some money and return to Anastasia in a better position.

Over coffee the next morning, I explained my decision to Stewart and Billy.

"Man, that beautiful chick?" Billy said.

"I know, but I need money. Anyway, I haven't exactly had good luck with beautiful women of late."

"At least write her a letter," Stewart said.

"Yeah, I guess I should."

"You taking the train?" he said.

"I don't know. I'll have to see what the train fare is. Just for meals alone, twenty bucks won't get me far."

"Hey, man. I'll buy you a ticket to Barcelona. How about that?"

"Come on, Stew. You don't have to do that."

"Fuck it. I've got the money and you don't want to be hitchhiking around this country. It's not like France. It really sucks."

I reluctantly agreed and Billy also helped with the ticket. The next train to Barcelona did not leave until midafternoon so they treated me to drinks in a bar next to the train station until it was time to go.

"Hey listen," Stewart told me out on the platform. "We're heading to Barcelona as soon as the festival is over. If you can find some way to survive until then, we'll see you in about four days."

"You're sure you don't want to hang around until then?" Billy said.

"No, I've got to deal with this money business."

"All right, then maybe we'll see you there," Stewart said with a slap on my back.

I boarded the train and found a seat by a window. Stewart and Billy were still standing there. I gave them a thumbs up and they did the same.

When the train finally lurched forward and started to pull away from the platform, we all waved until they were gone from view.

I looked forward with no idea what I was doing and a lot of feelings I couldn't seem to kick.

Nine

The high plain sloped down towards the distant sea from Pamplona in a patchwork of dry grassland and summer crops. We passed by small villages and peasants at work in the fields and bleak stone churches standing off by themselves. My window faced the Pyrenees and those once near peaks steadily receded as the train headed southeast, until they were but a distant rim of mountains.

Knowing the rough mileage between Pamplona and Barcelona, my mind played with estimates of train speed and time lost for stops and surmised that we would be arriving in Barcelona around twilight. The exact number of stops our train would make was something beyond my control but I felt reasonably confident in my assessment.

When my mind tired of that exercise, it moved on to anticipating the future and rearranging the past. I had a great many hopes and dreams and fears, all of them equally beyond my control.

Mainly, I had two women on my mind and wished one of them was there. Eva remained a powerful force but Anastasia now seemed much closer and dearer to my heart.

Roughly an hour out of Pamplona, the medieval castles of Odile reared up above the plain, bringing with them more dreams of knights and days of old. Fool that I was, I could not seem to kick my appetite for gallantry, riding off here and there, rescuing fair maidens.

When the train stopped at Odile, many people got off and boarded. We stopped several more times at villages along the way and eventually came to the city of Tudela on the Ebro River. More stone remnants of Spain's medieval past stabbed up into the skyline but all in all the town was considerably more modern looking than Odile.

As the day grew late and the many unexpected stops added up, my hopes of arriving in Barcelona by twilight had been steadily downgraded, until in the end, the train was pulling into Zaragoza at that fleeting hour, not Barcelona. By that point, I was willing to settle for arriving in Barcelona prior to midnight. I wasn't comfortable with blowing money on a room and dreaded the idea of searching out a park or the random woods in the wee hours of the morning.

We had been sitting there astride the platform in Zaragoza for some minutes, with the usual array of passengers disembarking and boarding, when a large contingent of army troops marched onto the train. Suddenly rifles were everywhere.

Being a fascist state, the tension among the passengers was visceral. Who knew if they were coming to drag you away?

A captain came aboard and announced that we were being diverted north to the city of Huesca. No further explanation was given. None of the passengers dared protest. The soldiers commandeered every empty seat and when those were filled, made themselves comfortable in the aisles.

As the train pulled out from the station, I overheard rumors of a terrorist attack by Basque separatists and that the troops were headed up north to deal with the revolt. Every ten miles or so, the train stopped again, letting more troops on, sometimes at another station, sometimes in the middle of nowhere. This went on repeatedly until it was well past nine by the time we pulled into Huesca. The waning moon had risen above the nearby Pyrenees, etching their shoulders in sylvan light. A dusting of snow accented the highest peaks.

The soldiers hurriedly disembarked. Orders were barked out. The sound of booted footsteps marched off into the night and, finally, the entire menace was gone.

Given the rugged mountain terrain, no one had thought to construct rail lines heading directly east from Huesca so the train was forced to turn back towards Zaragoza in order to reach Barcelona. I felt fortunate when the train pulled into the Barcelona station just past midnight. I had slept along the way but still felt exhausted.

Leaving the station, I caught the scent of the sea and knew it was close. I had hopes of grabbing a bite to eat and something to drink and went in search of those things before bothering with a place to sleep. A short distance up the street, I came across a small café that sold sandwiches and bought one on a croissant with smoked ham, cheese and marinated red peppers. Adding a beer and a small bottle of brandy from the liquor store next door, I headed on my way.

A few blocks farther up the street, I came across a night club and a group of young hipsters milling around out in front. In French, I asked if anyone knew of a place where I might camp nearby. Most of them stared. A few shrugged. With the backpack and a week of the road wearing on me, I wasn't their type. A guy who had been standing at the back of the group came forward.

"You looking for someplaces to sleep?" he said in English.

"Yeah, someplace to sleep."

He pointed north up the coast.

"You find a big park. Big, big park. Many trees. You sleep there and no police bother you."

He patted me on the back sympathetically.

"It's good for you. One night, no problemas."

I thanked him and headed on my way, saying a word of thanks for all kindhearted souls in this world.

In due course, I found the park and followed a path that wound off through the rolling lawns and woods. When I came to a knoll and what seemed like a suitable cluster of trees and shrubs, I settled in and made camp, safely hidden away from the world for one night.

Moonlight filtered down through the trees as I ate the sandwich and viewed my map. It did not look very far to Turin on paper. In a car it was one day. Hitchhiking, two days, or possibly three. Even at that, I had enough money to eat. Finding Eva's rich uncle was another thing. If he wasn't in Turin, I would have to travel down to the coast and search for him there. If that failed, I would try to find work, or steal, the same as men had been doing since the dawn of civilization.

Once I was done with the beer, I broke the seal of the brandy and had a drink. The warmth of the liquor felt good going down. I took off my boots, crawled into my sleeping bag and lay there thinking. My mind was back to wanting things it could not have and undoing things that were already done. I should have gone to Madrid. I should have done this. I should have done that.

When it got right down to it, I had foolishly chased a woman over to Paris, and that had left me stranded in Europe, nearly broke, and I simply had to deal with the situation as best I could.

It was a great pep talk that still left me lying all alone in a strange city, six thousand miles from home, with an ocean to cross in order to get back there. I poured a bit more brandy over those thoughts and sometime later fell asleep.

In the morning, I was startled awake by the sound of someone shouting in Spanish. With a peek through the shrubs, I saw it was a woman with her three small children, out enjoying the park. I relaxed again with the usual thoughts parading through my head.

A short while later, I was goaded into action. I needed to clean up and use the bathroom. I wanted coffee. Then it would be time to make some decisions. When to leave and which way to go.

I broke camp and moved a good distance away from the woman and her children before exiting the woods. Spotting a public bathroom, I headed in that direction. After a good wash and brush up, I marched off in the direction of the sea. The sun was out and had the feel of the tropics to it now.

I soon arrived to the boulevard across from Barcelona's main harbor. Looking south, wharves and great ships and heavy industry dominated the skyline as far as I could see. I turned north with the heavy scent of brine on the morning breeze.

A mile further on, I came to the statue of Columbus, quickly found a café back in a neighborhood of shops and restaurants, bought a coffee and pastry and wandered up a main boulevard, away from the sea. The street was shrouded by trees from end to end and cluttered with street vendors. I came upon hundreds of wooden cages hung from the trees, flitting with parakeets. Their songs filled the morning air. I saw capuchins for sale and every other imaginable thing and learned from a tourist that this makeshift bazaar was called Les Rambles.

I had stopped to rest on a shady bench and review my map again when a young blonde came along wearing a backpack. The backpack seemed massive on her petite form. She stopped in front of me and smiled. I smiled back.

"Are you an American?" I asked.

"No, German," she said with a heavy accent."

"But you speak English."

She made a gesture to say, not too well.

"Français ?"

"Oui. Français est mieux."

"Paul," I said, holding out my hand.

"Heidi."

I patted the bench so she dropped her pack and sat down next to me. I told Heidi that I had been robbed in Pamplona as a way of explaining my poverty. In a roundabout way, it seemed like an honest enough explanation for my problems.

Heidi announced that she had plenty of money. She had been saving up all year for this summer trip.

"You're hungry?" she said.

I gestured to say, no, I was fine.

"No, no. You come. I'll buy you something to eat."

We found a quiet café off the main boulevard and were soon talking over an omelet. Flamenco music poured out from a nearby restaurant.

Heidi wanted to go to Italy and thought we should do so together. It was her thought to head to Cinque Terra because someone had told her the Stones were making an album along the French coast somewhere and wouldn't it be great if we could find them? We could take photos and do an interview and sell it to the underground press.

As I sat there listening to Heidi and her plan, I realized that my infatuation for Anastasia's beauty had been just that, infatuation. With Heidi, there was something intellectual. She had a fine and lovely face but was also wonderfully smart and practical and I felt glad that she had walked into my life.

An hour later, we walked back out to Les Rambles and to a day that had grown unbearably hot. Even the canaries were singing wearily in their cages now.

"Do you know of a place where we can go swim in the sea?" I asked Heidi.

She nodded.

"Come. I'll show you."

We walked back down to the statue of Columbus, turned north up the coast and continued on through a park that bordered the inland side of road. After a mile trek, we stood opposite a row of classy looking white plaster buildings bordering the shoreline side of the boulevard, each with a carved wooden door, each door open to the very blue looking sea and all the colorful beach umbrellas beyond it.

"Come," Heidi said and reached for my hand.

"There?" I said. "Aren't they private clubs?"

"Yes."

"Who can afford that?"

"Oh, it's not that much. Come. It's only for one day."

"Why don't we go further up the coast? Isn't there someplace we can swim for free?"

"The next open beach is three miles away and it's where the sewer line dumps into the sea. Only the poor people and gypsies go there."

"Wow, okay. Yeah. I definitely don't want to go swimming there."

She smiled.

"Come. We can have a swim and a drink and then go up to sleep on the open beach tonight. It's a cool place to camp but you don't want to swim there."

She encouraged me again with her hand and we dashed across the road.

At the door, a very dark Spaniard with a mustache and white polo shirt reviewed us disdainfully, and probably would not have let us in except for Heidi's good looks and self-assured nature. That and two thousand pesetas got us through the door. I had watched ruefully as Heidi counted out

116

the money. For that sum, we were given a locker for our things, two sumptuous white towels and our choice of padded lounges.

"Jesus," I whispered to Heidi as we walked away with our towels. "We could have lived on that for days."

"Oh, don't worry. It's less than thirty American dollars."

Seeing my continued look of concern, she reached up and kissed me.

"Don't worry. We'll sell our story about the Rolling Stones for thousands of dollars and buy a house on the Riviera."

I chuckled over her pluck.

We were soon frolicking in the sea and then had drinks and sandwiches on our padded lounges and whiled away the afternoon. I tried not to have a care in the world, but I did. I tried to feel as if I belonged in such places but did not. It felt to me as if this dream would soon be swept away like etchings along the tide.

When the day grew late and a cool wind blew up from the sea, we showered and changed into fresh clothes and made our way back towards Les Rambles. Heidi took me to a club not far in from the coast and we sat there drinking wine and listening to music and talking until late with other young people who were out on the road.

It was a long hike up the coast to the public beach so I was greatly relieved when we were finally taking off our backpacks and making camp on the sand. The sea smelled of brine and there were fires off in the distance, where the gypsies had gathered for the night.

Heidi and I zipped our sleeping bags together and used our backpacks for pillows. It did not take us long to be consumed with our passions and we eventually fell asleep with the rest of our belongings gathered close by our heads.

In the morning, I was awakened by Heidi's hand, instantly saw what had happened and jumped to my feet. My Spanish boots were gone, along with my satchel and passport.

"Fuck," I said and looked off to where the fires had been in the night.

The gypsies were gone.

"What did they take of yours?" I asked Heidi.

"All my money."

"You didn't have traveler's checks?"

She shook her head.

"Oh no. And your passport too?"

"No. I had that in my pants."

I wandered around in a state, weighing my own loss. The boots, and my passport, and the satchel with my camera. My god. All the wonderful memories lost. Had it been possible, I would have hunted down every gypsy in the world right then and shot them.

I still had a pair of lightweight canvas shoes to wear and put them on. Heidi came over and held me.

"I need to stop at the German consulate," she said.

"Yeah, I know...I need to stop at the American consulate."

Spurred on by new anxieties, I pulled the money out of my pockets. There was barely ten dollars left. With no passport, I was trying to imagine the path forward.

"Well, let's go get a coffee and find our consulates," I said.

"I'm sorry," Heidi said.

"No, no. It's my fault. I should have looked out for you."

"No, it's my fault. I should have known better. You can't trust the gypsies."

"Well, it's done now. Let's go get some coffee and see what we can do."

It was a dismal march back to the city with little said between us. The German consulate was nearest so we shared a coffee and pastry and went there first. When Heidi explained the situation to the guard in front, he allowed us through the gate but she had to explain things again before we were allowed into the consulate itself.

I was asked to wait in the reception area while Heidi was led through a door. She returned half an hour later and waved for me to join her outside.

"What happened?" I said.

"They gave me a voucher for a train ticket and four hundred deutsche marks to get back home."

Four hundred deutsche marks was around a hundred dollars. I thought to ask Heidi how much she had lost but decided better of it. As effervescent as she had seemed the previous day, she now looked deflated.

"So, what are you going to do?" I asked.

"I don't know. Let's go see what they say at your consulate."

"All right."

It was another long walk across the city to the American consulate and they were not nearly as accommodating at the Germans. Heidi had to wait outside.

Inside, I explained the situation and was made to wait for nearly an hour. When I was ultimately led into an office by a young woman, I learned that they did not believe I was an American.

"What do I look like to you?"

"Well, frankly, not American."

I threw up my hands.

"Have you looked at yourself lately?"

"Yes and no but what does that have to do with anything? I mean, can't you tell by talking with someone that they're American?"

"There are some very clever people, looking to get into the United States."

I shook my head.

"Look, the Mets and Orioles were in first place, the last time I checked. Ohio State beat USC in the Rose Bowl. There was an oil spill in Santa Barbara in February. You want me to go on?"

"Mr. Daly. I have every reason to believe you're an American, but I also have to be prudent here. We'll give you a hundred dollars emergency funds and take your photo and you'll just have to wait until we can confirm your identity back in the States."

"And how long will that be?"

"I can't say for certain. As much as three weeks."

"Great. And what am I supposed to do in the meantime?"

"Well, fortunately you're in Barcelona with an abundance of activities to enjoy, cultural and so on."

"On one hundred dollars."

"Well, no one forced you to come to Europe with so little funds. And without a return ticket."

I was lectured further on what I could and could not do in the interim, which was basically, not to leave Spain, and perhaps not Barcelona, either. I was asked to sign for the one hundred dollars and allowed to return to the streets.

"So, what are you going to do?" I asked Heidi after explaining my situation.

"I've decided to go home."

Seeing my disappointment, she hugged me.

"Maybe you come holiday in Munich?"

"Well, I can't go anywhere right now. Why can't you just stay for a few days? We have enough money now between us."

"I'm sorry. I'm just too disappointed."

I bit my lip, fighting back tears.

"I'm sorry. It's all my fault," I said.

"No, no." Heidi brushed at my cheeks and kissed me. "You come to Munich once you have passport again, yes?"

I nodded. I wasn't sure that I would but I nodded.

"So? You walk me to the train station?"

"Of course, of course."

We headed back down towards the coast on foot.

"Let me buy you breakfast before I leave," Heidi said.

"It's okay. I have money now."

"No, please. I already have the train fare. I only need a little money to make it back to Munich. Okay?"

I shrugged and nodded.

After breakfast, we walked over to the station. The next train going north was leaving in fifteen minutes but headed for Frankfurt, not Munich. Upon further inquiry, Heidi was assured that she could catch a train going east at the German frontier.

She had written her contact information down on a piece of paper and handed it to me before stepping up to the landing. We kissed. The conductor was waving everyone onboard.

"You come see me, yes?"

I nodded.

She kissed me again with a forlorn smile, thrust 200 deutsche marks into my hand and disappeared inside before I could protest. A moment later, she appeared in one of the windows and waved. I waved back and stood there staring. We waved one last time as the train pulled away from the station and Heidi was gone.

Alone again, I walked out of the station and down a winding backstreet lined with medieval buildings. Wanting something to warm me in the night, I stopped at a liquor store and bought another bottle of brandy. With that in my backpack, I continued on along the backstreets of Barcelona and headed north up the coast. In time I came to the Jardí Botànic de Barcelona and hiked up to a knoll wooded with palm trees. With a view overlooking the city, I made myself comfortable back among the trees and opened the bottle of brandy. It felt warm and pleasant going down and quickly mellowed my wretched emotions.

I sat there considering the options. The extra money would help. With Heidi's two hundred deutsche marks, I now had a bit more than a hundred and fifty dollars. I could easily survive on that until the consulate provided me with a new passport but could not leave Spain in the meantime, which meant my life could not move forward. I could only look longingly at the map and Turin. I considered going back to Madrid but felt an aversion to that choice now that I could not explain.

There were canaries having a time of it in the palm trees above my head and the fronds whispered and the insects buzzed and I had soon fallen asleep.

I awakened a few hours later feeling alone and scared. I tried to control my emotions but could not. In my mind, I pictured a little cottage by the sea with a woman at my side and thought I would be very content with just those few things. Instead, all the women I had known were gone and everything I wanted in life seemed like a million miles away.

Filled with despair, I drank from the brandy and stared out over the city. The afternoon was growing late so I stirred and headed on my way. Finding a public restroom in the park, I cleaned up as best I could and changed clothes. I now had no fresh ones to wear but felt better for having cleaned up.

PARIS
UNKNOWN

Ten

On my way back down to the coast, I grew lost in a maze of narrow, winding backstreets and medieval buildings. Old women filled the doorways in the gathering dusk, black laced shawls over their heads, rosary beads turning in their hands, somber looks stolen at me as I passed by.

I came upon a set of stone steps leading down to a below street level tavern of some kind. Conversation and raucous laughter echoed up to the street. I paused there with the legs of patrons visible in the smoky light. I knew I was near the coast and my intended destination but decided to go down and have a beer.

It turned out to be a bar frequented by sailors. These were rough men in striped jerseys and knit caps, quick to laugh and equally quick to fight. The scent of beer and cigarette smoke mixed in the air. So did the tang of smoked sardines from a barrel sitting in the middle of the wooden floor.

A few of the men noticed my entrance but the laughter and revelry continued on as if I did not exist. I found a spot around one corner of the bar and ordered a beer. The sailor next to me was whispering something into a woman's ear just then. She laughed and her red blouse fell open, showing her breasts. The scent of her perfume mixed with the pall of smoke.

I saw a group of children run down the street, laughing. A ship's horn called out from the harbor. The shoes of various Spaniards went past the door with the urgency of that hour. Dreams of ships and distant journeys were in the air.

I paid for the beer, drank from it and reflected on what had brought me there. As Chris had said back in Paris, it was all about love and war, a war I had no interest in fighting and romances I couldn't seem to win.

I was a man without a passport, and seemingly without a country. Those were the most salient facts to my predicament right then.

For all its stark beauty, Spain had begun to depress me, from its fascism and black booted thugs to the grim mood of Catholicism that hung over everything else. Were all Spanish ladies required to repent at some age, I wondered? As far as I could tell, they all ended up wearing black shawls and counting rosary beads in doorways at dusk.

Not really expecting answers to these questions, I asked the bartender how much for a smoked sardine, learned that they were three pesetas, placed the appropriate amount of coins on the bar and took one from the wooden barrel behind me. It went down quickly, as did the rest of my beer. I called for another beer and cursed the gypsies under my breath. I had always been partial to free spirits, but those bastards had ruined it for me, leaving me stuck in Barcelona, with the freedom to walk where I chose during the day and drink where I liked in the evenings and little else. In my restlessness, I hungered to move on. I hungered to be anywhere in the world but where I was and realized in all of that just how much the road ahead of me was a means of escape from myself.

Missing Eva and Anastasia and Heidi in varying degrees, and wishing for the next woman to come along and fix me, I was about to continue down to the waterfront, where the young people gathered by the statue of Columbus at night, when a young man appeared alongside me and called to the bartender in a cockney accent.

"Cerveza, mate!"

With that, he spiked the hook attached to the end of his left arm squarely into the bar top and surveyed the patrons, me included. Dark hair tumbled down past his shoulders in loose curls. An earring glimmered through the hair. His shirt looked like something Errol Flynn would wear. With his wild, Byronesque good looks, he could have been in pictures.

The bartender came over, opened a bottle of beer, wiped the bar top around the hook, took the stranger's coins and departed.

"Cheers, mate," the man said to me and downed half the bottle. "The name's Mickey. Mick for short. Though there's some fond of calling me Captain Hook."

"Paul," I said with a nod his way.

"A bloody Yank 'e is. Well, 'eres to you."

With that, Mickey polished off the remainder of his beer and called for another one. I reviewed him again while he waited. When the second beer arrived, Mickey downed a good portion of that and wiped at his mouth with the sleeve of his pirate shirt.

"Pardon me for sayin' so, mate, but you look right prepared to piss in it."

I met his gaze for a moment, nodded and looked away. I wondered about the hook, and possibly where he had gotten the shirt. Beyond that, I didn't much care what he thought.

Aware that Mickey was staring at me, I looked at the hook lodged in the bar top and back up to his face.

"It is a device of many functions, me friend." Mickey worked the hook loose and admired it aloft. "The ladies, in particular, 'ave a liking for its polished gleam."

"What happened?" I asked.

Mickey drank from his beer.

"'Twas a fine mess, it was. Me being bloody smackered in a snowstorm and putting me wee head down to sleep on the first bench what comes along. Cold hearted nature did the rest. Me habit of sleeping sidewise is all that saved this right hand for posterity."

"You're British."

"Right smart, this one is. British as the bloody Queen."

"How long have you been in Barcelona?" I asked.

Mickey drank from his second beer and reflected.

"You 'ave me there. A singular question beyond me ability to recall. May you 'ave a finer recollection, mate."

"I've been here two days," I said.

"Right you are," he said, scratching his head with the hook. "I remember Pamplona and the bullfights but from there it all grows hazy."

"I was there."

"Then, mates we be. The last I remember, the bloody bastards had locked us into a ring with the lot of those bulls. Bloody mad, they were. Mad we were to be in there with them. Like to have horns of me own, I would." Mickey emphasized his point with an index finger held up to one side of his head. "A wee pissed on gin and the like. That's what it takes for that bit of foolery."

"Everyone was pissed in that town."

"Bloody fantastic, what? Pissed around the clock, we were. Did you see bloody Hemingway?"

"The imitator, yeah. Hemingway ruined the place."

"Aw, now, don't be such a sour lot. Drink up."

I met his bottle of beer with mine and drank.

I had grown lost in thought again when another sailor forced his way up to the bar, shoving Mickey closer to me. Both Mickey and I looked in his direction. The sailor smiled back as if to suggest that a fight would be a fine way to settle things, if that's what we wanted.

"Well, that'll be that, mate," Mickey said my way. "What do you say we 'ave a stroll along Les Rambles? See if some of this fine Spanish chickery has a liking for two dashing gents of the world."

I shrugged, downed the rest of my beer, grabbed my backpack and followed him up the stone steps and into the twilight. The old women with their black shawls and rosary beads had all disappeared, leaving the children to play alone along the winding, back street.

A few short blocks farther on, we came to Les Rambles and turned right down towards the sea. The marketplace stalls were mostly empty at that hour but the street still swarmed with people. Mickey went along beneath the trees, alternately dashing, dancing and leaping with a sudden rush at everyone who appeared in his way.

"Has the air of the deceased, what?" he said to a peevish looking old man with a cane.

The old man looked briefly startled then took a swing at Mickey with his cane. Mickey laughed and continued down the street, engaging people in this headlong manner, some of it well taken, some of it not, but he did not seem to care, one way or the other.

In this way I fell behind until we came to the crowded plaza around the statue of Christopher Columbus. Mickey had stopped there to survey the scene and wait for me. Across the boulevard from the plaza, the entire grassy promenade along the waterfront was teeming with people, young folks out carousing, families picnicking on blankets, lovers strolling hand in hand.

Mickey pointed out two Bavarian looking dolls seated at the base of the statue. They had backpacks at their feet and looked lost.

"A host they be to our gentle words, mate."

Mickey went over and bowed before them with a sweep of his hand. One of the young women giggled at Mickey's gesture. The other one looked put off by the sight of his hook and turned away. I stopped to take this in from several yards back.

"The name's Mickey and here be the noble Paul." Mickey waved emphatically for me to come forward. "At your service, fair ladies."

"I am Helga," the brighter of the two said with a giggle. "And this is Kristen."

Kristen looked again at Mickey's hook, glanced at me and quickly turned away.

"And what be the nature of your quandary, ladies? As, by the look on your faces, surely you have one."

"We sought to holiday in Ibiza tomorrow before taking the train home," Helga said. "But we miss early boat and now have only fourth-class for late boat. Dat means freezing all night on deck and Kristen, she don't want this."

Kristen said something sharply in German and the two of them argued. Meanwhile, Mickey was gesturing for me to give up the leather coat strapped to the outside of my pack.

"No, dat's okay" Helga said, seeing me start to untie it. "We have coat. Maybe we act too much like stupid tourist."

She laughed at herself and looked at Kristen. Kristen looked at us and away. Kristen was the beautiful one, but Helga had all the personality.

"What say we head off to Ibiza without delay," Mickey offered with one of his gallant gestures. "It's a fine, moonlit night. We'll buy a bottle of brandy. That and our noble hearts will surely keep you warm."

"I want to go," Helga said to Kristen.

Kristen shook her head with a look in the direction of the darkened port and the two women started arguing again.

I drifted away, thinking it was a dead end. Then, out of the crowd, I heard someone call my name and turned to find a man with a leather hat and dark shades crossing the plaza in my direction. He was nearly upon me before I realized it was Stewart.

"My man from Pamplona," he said with an embrace and pat on my shoulder.

"I didn't recognize you at first with the hat and sunglasses."

Stewart smiled.

"Incognito, baby. Incognito."

"I see."

I introduced him to Mickey.

"Oh yeah, I remember you from Barcelona," Stewart said. "In the plaza one night. Something to do with having your hook off."

"'Twas a lady's attempt to better examine me parts," Mickey said. "All in good fun."

Helga giggled.

"Oh, and this is Helga and Kristen," I said.

Steward bowed his head slightly at the two women.

"Ladies. So how was your trip?" he said to me.

"Rotten. The Guarda commandeered the train and routed us up through Huesca. Letting troops on and off every ten miles. It was pretty hard to relax with all those patent leathers crowding the aisles."

Two of them went by just then with their flat brimmed hats and automatic rifles slung over their shoulders. Everyone fell silent until they were gone.

"I've noticed a real uptick of those bastards in the past few days," Stewart said. "They arrested an American in Pamplona yesterday just for taking his shirt off in public."

"Aye, they're bastards, all right," Mickey said. "And the place is peppered with their dungeons. Right under our arses to this day."

Stewart nodded and looked back at me.

"So what were they after up in Huesca?"

"As best I could tell from listening to the peasants talk among themselves, something about the Basques making trouble."

Stewart nodded.

131

"It figures."

"Yeah. Anyway, it made for a bummer ride. I didn't get into Barcelona until well after midnight."

Stewart slapped me on the shoulder as if to commiserate.

"So what happened to Billy?" I asked him.

"Oh, he went down to see if he could find your ladies in Madrid. If things don't work out, I'm supposed to look for him here in three days. Did you ever write that letter?"

"No, hell. I'd completely forgotten about it. Not about her, though."

"Yeah, some beauty. I'm betting I'll never see Billy again."

"Yeah."

"So what else is new? Where are you crashing?"

I told him about my first night and Heidi and the experience with the gypsies.

"All those photos we took, man. I'm bummed out about that more than anything else."

"Yeah, shit, but no use in pouting. What are you folks cooking up?"

"Gentlemen," Mickey said. "Seeing that these lovely ladies have an expedition to Ibiza in mind, I say we offer our gallant protection, being they are but poor, defenseless things in the world."

"Get off it," Stewart said with a laugh. "Is he for real?"

"As real as this hook, mate."

"All right, all right. No offense intended. Are you going, Paul?"

"I can't. I'm not supposed to go anywhere until I get my new passport."

"No cause for concern, me friend, as there be no customs for Spanish vessels arriving on Ibiza."

"Hell, I'm up for the adventure," Stewart said.

"No customs?" I repeated to Mickey, not entirely trusting him.

"Not port to port, mate. Even these Spanish bastards will trust you that far. I say let's be off."

He brandished his hook skyward with a flourish and the three of us looked collectively at the ladies. Kristen glanced at the darkened port again and failed to budge. Mickey spoke aside to us.

"How does this sound, mates? You go take care of the tickets and I'll see if I can cajole the chickery, here."

"Sure, take your best shot," Stewart said.

With a smile and nod at me, we dashed across the busy boulevard.

"Is he always so full of shit?" Stewart said on the other side.

"I don't know. I just met him. I'm guessing too much Shakespeare."

"Or too many Errol Flynn movies."

"Maybe that too."

Stewart imitated Mickey and we laughed.

A damp sea mist was drifting across the harbor as we made our way into the maze of wharfs and warehouses. I looked back once and saw Mickey still talking to Kristen and Helga.

"Forget it," Stewart said. "I've got my money on that pirate running off with them alone."

"I don't know. I don't think he's that type."

"Yeah, we'll see."

We located the ticket office and inquired about the fares. It was a hundred and forty pesetas to Ibiza. Stewart and I dug out our money and bought two tickets.

On our way down the wharf to the ferry, I heard Mickey calling out. He had come alone.

"No luck, huh?" Stewart said.

"I told them we leave on the tide and off they went. It was that sour one, Kristen. Spent her whole life sucking on lemons, she has."

"Oh well, we're off," Stewart said. "Are you coming?"

"Captain Hook at your service, mates."

"Well, captain. It's a hundred and forty for the passage."

"A pittance for the pleasure of sailing, that is."

Mickey hurried off pulling pesetas from his pocket.

"Sad to be sailing off without that bottle of brandy," he said in catching up with us.

"I've got what's left of a pint in my pack."

"Then our sails be trimmed, mates."

We had come to the ferry and a line of people waiting to board.

"Have you ever been to Ibiza?" I asked Mickey.

"Aye, but it's a tourist trap, mate. Now Formentera. There's a kindly destination all its own. A more tranquil jewel of sand, pine groves and turquoise seas you've never seen. Clear as the sky, the water is, and the sand as white as your bottom."

"And plenty of cold beer, I hope," Stewart said.

"Plenty of that. And naked women, too."

"You'll see my bare ass in the turquoise sea, all right," Stewart said.

He showed his ticket to the porter and headed up the gangway. Mickey did the same.

"What about the other islands?" I said, bringing up the rear.

"I'm telling you, mate. Formentera's where we want to be."

"Let's just get to Ibiza and see how things look," Stewart said.

On the upper deck, we found three unoccupied seats and settled in. The whistle blew some minutes later and the ship backed away from the dock. We had soon cleared the harbor break and entered open seas. The sea mist steadily gathered on our clothes and faces.

"A bit of that brandy would do us good right about now," Mickey said.

I dug out the bottle and we passed it around while swapping tales. The harbor lights steadily receded until they had completely disappeared below the horizon.

"Across the Seven Seas," I said.

"Aye, and what a fine night it is to be on them."

"Ulysses sailing for home," Stewart said.

"Hear me, mates. It's all a bit of Greek mythology. And we have our Paul here to thank for this bit of spirits to cut the fog."

"And all your crap," Stewart said.

"You'll miss me yet, mate. Mark my word."

"I look forward to the opportunity."

The two men laughed.

"But listen. It be the truth. We'll all be fine and warm on Ibiza in the morning. The day's rise as dry as the Sahara and the sea swallows you as sweetly as a tub of water on an English summer's day."

"A fine thought," Stewart said.

"A fine thought, indeed." Mickey shook his head. "And to think of all the war and pillaging going about these days. We're in the shade here."

At hearing the word war, I looked off across the sea. You wanted to forget 'Nam but you couldn't. If you were a young man in America, it was always there to haunt you. You were either about to be drafted, or already had been, or were just damned lucky that your number had come up big instead of small.

"Listen, mate," Mickey said, having seen my mood darken. "It's not so much a matter of places but of disposition, so let's cheer up."

"I'll cheer up when you cut the bullshit," Stewart said.

"It's all in fun, mate. All in fun. Like these tourists we'll see on the morning dock. How I love the bloody bastards. Bermuda shorts and socks. A Kodak about their necks. Five hundred quid for their dream vacation and they'll look lost as sheep in the rain the minute we get there."

"And what's your plan?" Stewart said.

"Straight on to a bar, mate. What else be there?"

"Sounds good to me, you bloody bastard."

"That I am, that I am, and proud of it."

We all grew tired and cold as the night wore on and finally fell asleep.

Shortly after dawn, I was startled awake by the ship's horn. Stewart and Mickey were already standing at the deck rail. I got up to join them. The morning was dry and clear with a light breeze.

We had entered a small harbor with ancient stone works. White pleasure craft dotted the turquoise waters. Buildings cascaded down the hill behind the harbor, the hill sprinkled with palms trees and shrubbery and dominated by the walls of a medieval castle. From several balconies, laundry flapped in the morning breeze.

"I'm guessing the Romans," Stewart said.

"You'd be right," Mickey said. "Metellus gave the place a once over. Back in 123 B.C, as I remember it. Did a nice job on the harbor after he had knocked the locals around a bit."

"And you were here, I suppose," Stewart said.

"No. Just read about it in a book. Ah, but it's all in passing."

"Those goddamned walls look to be more than in passing to me."

"I'm famished," I said.

"What does that have to do with Roman legions?"

"I'm hungry, that's all."

"A beer with some eggs and bangers will do nicely," Mickey said.

With the ship anchored, the three of us made our way down to the dock.

"We're a fine lot of tourists in the morning sun."

"Just show me to a cold beer," Stewart said.

"Right this way, mates."

Mickey led us up a broad set of stone steps to street level and into a small bar. As Stewart was paying for three beers, I opened the windows to the morning breeze. An Algerian radio station was playing Arabic music. The French proprietor pointed at his collection of American music and welcomed us to put on any record we liked. Stewart thumbed through them and chose a Jefferson Airplane album. The three of us ordered breakfast and cleared our heads with the cold beer. The world was right there through the open windows.

" 'At's right," Mickey shouted down at the tourists milling around the harbor. "Get yourselves all organized for the day."

Several of them looked up our way.

"Makes you want to get bloody smackered, eh mate?"

"I've got my money on that being your mother down there," Stewart said. "The one in the checkered polyester shorts."

"Mum!" Mickey shouted out. "I'd know you anywhere. By the veins in your pasty legs."

Mickey propped his legs up on the extra chair.

"And not a bloody thing to do all day."

"If we're going to Formentera, shouldn't we be arranging our passage," I said.

"Here 'e goes again, bein' a bloody tour guide."

Our breakfast was served and Stewart joined us at the table.

"Well, it would be nice before nightfall."

"You 'ave something against darkness, mate?"

"Yeah. I like to be in my cave before the lions come out."

"Bloody sage. If we were Paleolithic."

"It's a fair question," Stewart said, looking up from his plate. "How do we get to Formentera?"

"We swim, and you can start anytime."

"Not your strong suit, eh mate," Stewart said, imitating Mickey.

"Easy on me, lads, easy. We hire a fisherman. There'll be dozens of them converging on the port any minute now."

"How much do they charge?" I said.

"A few pence. The more on board, the better it goes on our purse strings."

"He'll sink the boat trying to save a quid," Stewart said.

I ate in silence while the two of them bantered back and forth, my thoughts on three women, a missing passport and one rich uncle.

When the plates were cleared, we ordered more beers. The album had stopped playing so the proprietor turned the Algerian station back on. We sat talking quietly, waiting for the fishermen to come in from sea and enjoying the morning breeze through the windows.

Eleven

Shortly after ten, the first fishing boat motored back into port. We watched the men onboard tying off at the dock.

"So, what now?" Stewart asked Mickey.

"Best to wait. The better the price if there's competition."

"You're in charge."

"Just leave it to me, mates."

Others fishing boats soon followed. Mickey waited until there were a half dozen tied up along the stone seawall before going out the door. The morning breeze had stalled, leaving the harbor waters calm and glassy under the hot sun.

Mickey approached one of the crews as they were unloading their catch. The owner glanced up while continuing to work. Following their brief conversation, Mickey marched back up the stone steps to the bar and looked in through the open windows.

"He's off for a bite to eat and a snog with the missus. A few hours now and he'll be back to give us a lift."

"So how much?"

"Seventy pesetas a head."

That was a bit less than one American dollar.

"All right," Stewart said. "We won't make you swim then."

"Bloody wanker," Mickey said and came around to the door.

Before noon, the fisherman began to reappear and the tourists converged around them and their boats. By the time everything had been arranged with our skiff, there were eight of us aboard and it sat low in the water.

We cleared the harbor with the sea running high and a mist in our faces. With every glance off the waves, another bit of spray splashed up from the bow. I had one hand in the blue water and an old sea shanty in my heart.

Formentera grew larger and larger on the horizon, from a low spit of land above the whitecaps to forested hills rising up on either side of the isthmus. The fisherman headed for a crescent shaped bay on our right. Inside the breakwater, the water was aquamarine and dotted with pleasure craft. The fisherman pulled up to a quay and steadied the boat as everyone disembarked. With all of us offloaded, he quickly turned back out to sea and motored off without a word.

"This way, mates," Mickey said. "It's a bit of a march across to the lee side but that's where all the festivities be."

Stewart's hat blew off and he went chasing after it.

"Let's hope like hell there's a lee side," he said, coming back.

We followed a road out of town.

"It's a bit of a hike, all right," Stewart said when we had been walking for half an hour.

"We be close, mates. Here it is now, the secret passageway."

We were astride a small bay with a handful of docks and pleasure craft when Mickey turned inland along a narrow trail. The wind quickly diminished as we pushed through some dense shrubbery and moved away from the coast. Farther on, the trail turned to sand and the sand was warm beneath our feet.

"What do you think, mate?" Mickey said to me over his shoulder.

"I wasn't expecting the Bataan Death March."

"Trust me, mate, it's a poet's dream, where we be headed. Not all is practicality."

"Just get me to a seat and a cold beer," Stewart said from the rear.

At times the trail was exposed to the brilliant sun. At others, we passed through olive groves cut through with ancient stone walls.

Farther on, we came upon a white plaster home off to the left of the trail, partly obscured by several palm trees. The deep-set entrance of the house was additionally shaded over by a wooden arbor and vines had grown wild over both the arbor and house. A woman with short black hair and fair skin sat out in the shade of the arbor, reading a book. She brushed the hair back from her face and waved as we approached.

"How much for the flat?" Mickey shouted out from the grove.

"Are you paying in pounds or American dollars?" she called back with a British accent.

"Whatever you like!"

"It's not for sale but come along if you like!"

"She's a bloody Brit," Mickey said. "

"Bloody brilliant, this one," Stewart said.

"Aye, you're still on me about those two birds. I can feel it in me bones."

"Yeah, you blew that one all right."

"Well, one in the hand is worth two in the bush, as they say."

"Mickey claims you're the Queen," Stewart said as we neared the woman.

"What on earth are you talking about?"

"Nothing really. Just a bit of silly British humor."

"Well, then, perhaps I'm not British after all...The name's Anne," she added and held out her hand.

We introduced ourselves all around and accepted Anne's offer to sit down.

"Mickey here will do the interpreting," Stewart said.

Anne laughed.

"Well, you must have had a long day," she said. "Even I can interpret that. Would any of you care to use the facilities?"

Each of us took advantage of Anne's offer and in due course came to sitting together in the warm shade. I noted the Durrell novel in Anne's lap.

"Do you like him?" she asked.

"I remember the start to *Mount Olive*. Riveting, but it quickly went downhill from there. Who's doing the major's wife and all that?"

"Hankies and parlors and all such naughty nonsense," Stewart said.

"Careful, I'm English and have a fondness for hankies and parlors."

There were smiles.

"Lovely little place," I said. "How do you find something like this?"

"That's the domestic in him," Mickey said. "Last night, we were a fine lot of pirates on the tide. Now we'll be 'aving English gardens and the likes."

"All ladies prefer sheets and fine linens," Anne said.

"Right you are. 'Ave a go at it, then, mate."

Anne studied us, smiling.

"I'm expecting some friends over this evening. Wine and cheese and such. Why don't you join us?"

"Aye, and after that, I'll be on the wind," Mickey said. "For it's wind what fills me sails."

"And BS what provides the wind," Stewart said.

"Well, we've plenty of both," Anne said amidst the laughter.

In the silence that followed, I stole another glance her way, allured by this woman in her thirties and the aura of hearth and home. My young life had been blown all about by the wind. I hadn't the slightest notion what it would be like to settle down with someone and share a home.

"Let's go find this bar of yours," Stewart said to Mickey.

"Yes, you'll find the beach and the little cabana lovely," Anne said. "It's covered with palm fronds and the Spaniard who runs it has a fine collection of American records. Francisco's his name. Try one of his daiquiris."

Stewart was on his feet and skipping off.

"Haiquiri daiquiri dock, three drinks and I'll be socked."

Stewart and his impromptu song disappeared into the olive grove

"We're off then," Mickey said, getting to his feet.

"Maybe we'll see you tonight," I said to Anne.

"Or soon. You'll find life is quite measured here. As there's nowhere to go, there's not much point in hurrying."

"Bye for now, then."

"So long."

I hesitated.

"You'd better hurry," she said. "Before your friends disappear on you."

Anne laughed at her own joke. I waved again and ran to catch up with the others.

Nearer to the sea, we entered a pine grove. Off through the trees, a white sand beach and turquoise sea were visible and the blue sky peeked down through the pine boughs above our heads. At the edge of the grove, we came across bedrolls and signs of campfires. I picked a secluded spot for my own campsite and deposited my backpack.

The grove emptied out onto the sand fifty feet farther on. The bar was a round cabana with a palm fond roof and stood a hundred feet back from the water's edge. A mélange of international drifters surrounded it, many of them dark-skinned — Arabs, Africans and Indians among the crowd — but a great many were Caucasians too. Laughter, rock & roll music and a buzz of conversation carried on the wind.

Francisco, a breezy looking Spaniard with black hair, dark skin and white teeth welcomed us to his bar and we were soon lost in the merriment of the moment. Some hours later, with sunset approaching, a cool wind blew up from the sea.

"Meet Gunga Din," Mickey said, coming around the cabana with a dark-skinned fellow under his arm.

"I am Sunseray," he said with the Namaste sign. "But you may call me Sun."

"Bloody Gunga Din, 'e is."

Sun smiled good-naturedly, uncertain what to make of both Mickey and the reference to Gunga Din. As was typical of Sunseray's race, his dark, watery eyes seemed to wrap around his forehead.

"How about a portrait then?" Mickey said, reaching for a camera inside Sunseray's woven bag. "Smile, the lot of you."

I placed my arm around Sunseray's shoulder and Stewart stood in back with the two ladies he was courting.

"Please, be most careful," Sun said, retrieving his camera. "I have only a few frames remaining and shall miss the moment."

Sunseray wandered down closer to the water's edge.

"Says he takes a snapshot of every sunset...Get on with you then!" Mickey called out. "The fiery orb is about to set!"

As the sun neared the sea, everyone around the bar grew hushed. Sunseray stood there with camera poised and took his photo just as the sun kissed the horizon. Once the last reddish glow had disappeared, there were cheers and the festivities resumed.

"Show me," I said to Sun as he returned.

"I shall do that, thank you."

He pulled a thick envelope out of his bag and set it on top of the bar top.

"Here is one of Madagascar. And Kenya. And that is Tangier, I believe. Ah, Marrakech. There are many, many more. Please, do enjoy them."

Mickey looked over my shoulder.

"All the same as the back of me hand, they are. I say it calls for a drink."

He ordered a fresh daiquiri. I sat there flipping through the photos as evening descended over the gathering and the sea swished quietly at the shore. When I looked up again, Stewart had disappeared, along with his two lady friends. My thoughts turned to Anne and that age-old hunger.

"Think I'll go see what's happening up at Anne's place," I told Mickey.

"Good luck with the queen, then."

I nodded and headed for my campsite back among the trees. The scent of the sea followed me and mingled with the scents of pine and charcoal from last night's campfires.

I brushed my teeth and rolled out my sleeping bag to mark my campsite before leaving.

At Anne's place, I found a small gathering of men seated around the living room. Anne introduced me to all. I took the only seat left, beside her. The wine and conversation flowed. I listened for the most part. These were all men of the world, at least twice my age, some even older. I felt very diminished and awkward in comparison.

Peter, an older, gray-haired man in shorts and sandals lit up a pipe with hashish. It went around the room several times. There was coughing and eventually much laughter.

"How are you finding things so far?" Anne asked me amidst the now irreverent conversations.

"It seems like a cool life. Bathing in the sea and daiquiris for breakfast. I wish I could stay."

"Why don't you?"

"I don't know. How do you survive?"

"By breathing," she said with a smile. "Seriously, I do a bit of exporting and grow what I can. I've heard of people selling crafts to the tourists, though there aren't many of those, thank god. Others have gotten on with the fishermen. A bit of this and a bit of that, you see. You've money, I presume?"

"Not much."

I explained about being robbed and the passport business.

"Well, let's hope you give it a go," Anne said. "We'd be delighted to have you. There's always one place or another for rent, right Peter? I believe you had mentioned seeing a house up on the other end, near San Francisco?"

He looked up from his conversation with a smile.

"That house you had mentioned?" Anne repeated.

"Oh, yes. Thirty-five thousand a month, I believe it was."

Anne looked at me hopefully. I shrugged. Five hundred a month, American dollars. Christ. Where was I going to get that kind of money?

"Well, you can always save your money and stick to camping while you get a foothold," she encouraged me.

Sure. Chin up and all that. What I wanted from her was an invitation. We'd fall in love and live happily ever after.

Seeing that that wasn't in the cards, at least not for one night, and that Anne's friends weren't about to leave any time soon, I headed back to the beach a short time later. Along the shore, faces glowed in the light of campfires. The sound of guitars and flutes and makeshift percussion filled the night. I smelled the pungent aroma of more hashish on the evening breeze.

Back at Francisco's bar, I found Stewart with his two lady friends. Mickey was playing his cards on the free one. Stewart called out my name and ordered me a fresh daiquiri.

"Where have you been, old boy?"

I explained my trip up to Anne's place.

Suddenly, Mickey stood up from his bar stool and threw out his arms.

"Would you look at it, mates. The bloody Milky Way. And what a fine tribe of people we are tonight, gathered as it were on the shores of eternity."

148

Mickey's declaration was met with cheers all around. He sat down next to me, seemingly touched by his own words.

"I tell you, mate. The infinite stars be in me mind and the Seven Seas in me heart. Though I can't explain it."

"I don't think anyone can, Mick. The feelings are lost in trying."

He put his arm around me with a smile.

"Believe me, mate. You're a fine one to 'ave along."

"The same to you."

"A toast to the universe, then."

"A toast to the universe."

We drank.

"Say, mate," Mickey said aside to me, as if confiding a great secret now. "Take me right but there be a splendid opportunity here on this island…For the willing."

"What's that?"

He leaned over further and whispered in my ear.

"There's a motley crew rowing this hashish ashore. From Morocco, they say."

He pulled back to look in my eyes and leaned in again.

"It's a smart business, I tell you, and a handsome profit to be made, sporting it back to Barcelona."

Mickey finished his daiquiri and met my eyes.

"So what do you say, mate?"

"I say I've got enough troubles already. And so do you."

"Just the same, put your mind to it overnight. And keep this tight under your bonnet."

I finished my drink and found myself yawning.

"Christ, I'm exhausted. I need to get some sleep." I stood up from my barstool. "I'll see you guys in the morning."

"It's front and center at the shore first thing," Stewart said. "Bring your own bar of soap. Then it's daiquiris for breakfast."

"We'll start with the bath and see how things go from there."

I saluted to them and headed down the beach.

Late into the night, lying back among the pine trees in my sleeping bag, I heard the music from Francisco's records and laughter around his bar, those sounds mixing with people playing guitars and flutes and singing around various campfires. The fires flickered along the beach, like fireflies through the trees.

Memories came of all the women I had ever known and loved, with wishes that one of them was there to comfort me now. Then suddenly all my thoughts coalesced around Anne. Not so strangely, the idea of an older woman in my life was comforting, a sense that she could fix everything—my poverty, my despair, my complete lack of direction in this world.

Much later, people began to drift up from the shore and settle into their separate camps. I went to sleep to the sounds of people making love back among the trees.

I was awakened in the morning by people frolicking down in the sea. The white sand was brilliant through the pines, the air dry and warm, the sea turquoise-blue and sparkling. I lingered in my sleeping bag for a spell, going over and over the same things I had been going over and over about in the night.

When I heard Stewart calling my name urgently, I got up and into my swimsuit and walked down to the sea with a bar of soap.

"We're all scrubbed up and ready to go," he said, seeing me appear.

"Go where?"

"Right there," he said, pointing at the bar.

"You bastard. I thought you meant you were taking off."

"We'll be taking off, all right."

"Bastard."

I dove into the crystal-clear water and felt heavenly after two days on the road. Following a good scrub, I swam for a bit and headed back to my makeshift camp. Sporting a pair of shorts, my striped shirt and canvas shoes, I headed over to the shade of Francisco's cabana. It had already grown hot, if anyone needed an excuse for having daiquiris before breakfast. I ordered one and settled in next to Mickey. We were a groggy looking lot with our sea washed hair and bloodshot eyes.

Mickey had his gaze fixed on a nut-brown beauty swimming naked offshore. She dove into the aquamarine water, as sleek as a dolphin, and resurfaced with black hair draped about her apple sized breasts.

"A siren for me ardent desires, she is."

"I can see that."

"No doubt some Abyssinian treasure, what?"

"I would go with that one, yeah."

"Ah, 'tis an ancient wind what blows amongst the columns of me manly emotions. As sweet a wind as ever I've felt."

"Very poetic, Mickey. You should tell her that."

"I shall. I shall indeed."

He remained silently enraptured. I drank and worked on own plans for seduction. By the second daiquiri, Anne and I were starting a family.

After much delay, the object of Mickey's desires finally strolled out of the sea, dried off with a sky-blue towel, wrapped it about her brown body and continued up to the bar. Seeing

Mickey stare, she gave him a sardonic smile, placed a hand on the bar and called out to Francisco.

"Hey, partner! How's about throwing me a beer here. I'm dying of thirst."

Hearing her Brooklyn accent, I had to choke back a laugh.

"What's your problem, pal?" the woman said.

"Oh, nothing, nothing. We were just on the subject of long-lost Abyssinian treasures when you walked up."

"Long lost what? Hey, Francisco. Get this guy another drink before he goes over."

I held up my hand to the ever smiling Francisco and looked at Stewart. He too was holding back his mirth.

"What do you say we head over to Anne's place?"

"Yeah, sure. I'm game."

We started across the fine, white sand, leaving Mickey behind to try his luck with the Abyssinian beauty.

"And what's wid *yur* stare, already?" I heard her saying "Hey, Francisco. You know somethin' about this one-armed bandit here?"

"Good luck," I called back to Mickey as we disappeared among the pines.

All the way over to Anne's place, the two of us were doing a schtick with Brooklyn accents.

With Anne's home in view, we hopped over the last stone wall and dashed from the shade of the olive grove to the shade of her front arbor. The day was blazingly hot and Anne's friends Peter and Charles were fanning themselves inside on her couch.

I explained Mickey's adventure to a great deal of laughter.

"So, were you two off looking for a house then?" Anne said in the silence.

Stewart looked at me like this was news.

"You planning to settle down or something?" he said.

I shrugged.

"Well it's too damned hot to go anywhere. If anything, let's head into town for supplies and leave it at that."

"Peter here has a motor scooter you can use," Anne said. " But why don't you relax for now. Stay awhile and have a bite to eat with us."

"Thanks," I said. "Do you mind if I use your rest room?"

"Oh, not at all, but be careful. The plumbing's not much."

I used the toilet, tried to do something with my hair and returned to find everyone had moved to the kitchen. I went out to offer my help. There were eggs and sausage frying in a pan and bread and melon being sliced. Butter, jam and orange juice were already waiting on the table.

After a fine meal, Peter lit up the obligatory bowl of hashish. In the stillness, we sat and dreamed. Flies performed lazy aerial ballets in the center of the room and voices and laughter carried up from the sea.

"Anyone up for a swim and a daiquiri at Francisco's?" Anne said later on.

As a form of general assent, all of us nodded and rose up out of our chairs. Anne went off to change. The rest of us gathered under the arbor out front. When she reappeared, we hurried across the sun scorched clearing and into the shade of the groves and from there made a final dash across the hot sand to the shore. After the swim we had daiquiris and after the daiquiris another swim. This kept on all day, until the wind turned back from the sea and a cool breeze blew across the island.

When there was talk of leaving, I grabbed Anne's free hand under the bar top and whispered in her ear.

"Please stay."

Her friends were already up and starting to move off.

"Coming?" Peter said.

"Oh, it's simply too lovely to leave," Anne said with a smile.

"You'll be safe then."

"Of course, Peter, of course. I have Paul here to walk me home."

Peter hesitated with a look at me and drifted off with Charles in the arid twilight. I met Anne's eyes.

"So, what are we doing here?" she said.

"Another daiquiri?"

"Oh surely you can come up with a better excuse than mere decadence."

"Like you said, it's simply too lovely to leave?"

"Ha. Well, you have me there."

"It's irrefutable logic," Stewart said from over my shoulder.

"Irreputable," Anne said.

"It doesn't count if it's not a word," Stewart said.

"Snobby Columbia undergraduate."

While their banter continued, I had Francisco pour us another round.

"To irreputable logic," I said when the drinks arrived.

Anne and I toasted. I was back to staring into her hazel-green eyes. Her right hand had reached out absentmindedly to explore mine. I continued staring.

"You're quite the romantic, Paul," she said with a sip of her drink.

"What? I just love looking into your eyes. It seems like the mystery of the whole universe is hidden inside there somewhere."

"Indeed."

"What? You don't believe me."

"Oh, I don't know…"

"Or you think I'm just a wild young man."

"Well, there's that, yes."

"So tame me."

She scoffed sweetly and drank from her daiquiri, her eyes still locked on mine. We had been lost in our mutual gaze for a minute when Stewart spoke up.

"Well, I'll be a witness."

We all looked up to find Mickey appearing out of the pine grove just then, holding hands with his Abyssinian princess.

Twelve

"The Abyssinian princess arrives," I whispered into Anne's ear.

Mickey strolled up beaming. His princess called out in her thick Brooklyn accent.

"Line 'em up here, Francisco!"

Anne pressed her nose firmly to mine, as if to better hold back her laughter. Francisco poured two glasses full from his pitcher of daiquiris and Mickey's lady took one.

"And what are you two love birds smiling about over here?" she said with a sip of her drink.

Anne still had her nose touching mine. It was a race to see who would burst out laughing first, and I lost. I backed away and slapped Mickey on the shoulder to diffuse the tension.

"So how are you doing, my friend?"

"My main sails be trimmed, mate. How be the fates treating you?"

"Good, good…And I'm sorry, your name is?"

"Barbara."

"Paul," I said with a laugh. "And this is Anne."

"How ya doin'?" Barbara said to Anne "They're gonna have to lock him up one of these days for…"

She spun an index finger at her forehead and nodded at me.

"…ya know?"

Anne looked at me with lips pressed together.

"I gather you're from New York then," she said to Barbara.

"And I gather you're from England…Amazing how we can figure this stuff out, isn't it?"

Anne laughed.

"Yes. Yes, it is quite amazing, when you think of it."

The general revelry soon carried Barbara and Mickey off to the other side of the cabana and I was back to staring into Anne's eyes.

"You'll wear yourself out like this, you know."

"No," I said. "I don't think so."

Anne sipped her daiquiri with a look over the glass.

"You'll have to explain in more detail exactly what it is that you're seeing some time."

"I would love to. Maybe tonight?"

Anne looked at me askance.

"Perhaps."

We had been sitting there for a minute or so, touching hands and enjoying the lovely evening when the hollow notes of a wood flute carried on the wind. With a look over my shoulder, I saw a very dark-skinned African fellow making his way down the beach, the flute to his lips and a colorful collection of V-neck shirts strung handily over his shoulder.

As he neared the cabana, our newest vagabond called out "Greetings, greetings!" to all and hung his brightly colored cotton shirts from the edge of the overhang. A number of folks held their drinks up to him and resumed their conversations without losing a beat. The man ordered a drink and returned to playing his flute while he waited. I smiled at him and thumbed through his shirts. Each one of them had a unique mandala across the front, created by a tie dye method of some sort.

"Befitting your skin," Anne said when I held up one of the shirts to my chest.

"What do you mean?"

"Any more sun and you'll turn into a nut."

The African fellow lowered his flute with a big gold-toothed smile.

"You are raja blue daddy. Prince with a heavy heart."

His words came with the thick accent typical of his continent. I gave Anne a quizzical look.

"He said it, not me."

Stewart suddenly reappeared from somewhere down the beach and slapped me on the shoulder.

"He means for you to cheer up."

"Yeah, sure. And you? Where are the two dolls?"

"Gone back to Barcelona. And home. The fall semester is calling us all."

It wasn't calling to me. There was nothing I wanted back there. Eva? A war? Things one and all I now preferred to forget.

Stewart slapped me on the shoulder again and ordered a drink.

"All right," I said to the African fellow. "What's your name?"

"Djimon. The man of stout heart."

"Okay, well. Raja blue daddy here likes this shirt. How much?"

"For you, 350 pesetas. Five dollars American."

I looked from the shirt to Anne. She shrugged.

"Okay. It's a deal."

I paid Djimon and immediately exchanged my shirt for the new one. The sleeves hung loosely from my arms at three-quarter length. When I held them out, the new shirt was greeted with general cheers.

Djimon smiled his gold-toothed smile and went back to playing his flute. Stewart had disappeared again. I looked back at Anne.

"Raja blue daddy," I said quietly.

"The name befits you. As does the shirt."

"In lieu of doing my laundry."

"No doubt you'd fancy doing a load at my place."

"There are a number of things I'd fancy doing over at your place, dear Anne."

That got me another one of her smiles over the daiquiri.

"Laundry being high on the list. I've been on the road for what...ten days now? Something like that and it's started to sink in on me how uncivilized a man can become."

Anne finished her daiquiri and set the glass down on the bar top with her gaze locked on mine.

"You did say you were walking me home, old boy, didn't you?"

"At your service, fair princess."

"And? What of your humble abode?"

"Shall I bring it with me?"

"There was talk of doing your laundry."

"There was."

"So? Shall we gather your things first?"

"Sure."

In sync, Anne and I slipped off our barstools and offered an informal goodnight to all.

On our way down the beach, we held hands. The warm, clear water lapped gently at our feet. The night air was laced with campfire smoke and that sharp scent followed us back among the pines. Anne waited while I rolled up my sleeping bag.

"Any port in a storm," I said.

"I am *not* any port in the storm, young man."

"Sorry. I was referring to my lodgings here, not yours."

She accepted my kiss on the forehead and we started off through the grove together.

Back at Anne's cottage, she did not bother with turning on the lights.

"Put your pack down anywhere," she said. "We'll deal with the laundry in the morning."

I made myself comfortable on the sofa and watched her go about lighting candles. When she returned and settled in next to me, the walls were dancing with light and shadow.

"Lamps would have been a bit jarring, don't you think?"

"I'm with you all the way."

"Raja blue daddy."

"That's me."

"What would you say to a bowl of hashish?"

"I'd love it."

"I thought you would."

"I grew up getting high."

"Grew up?"

"Well, since I was sixteen."

Anne chuckled.

"All two long years of your grueling adult journey."

"It does seem like quite a bit longer somehow."

"Everything does when you're high."

I smiled and watched Anne dig out her hash and pipe.

"Mickey was talking about taking some back to the mainland to make a buck."

Anne darted a glance my way while loading the pipe.

"I would be very, very wary of going down that path, Paul."

"Why? Do they search you back in Barcelona?"

"Generally, no, but there's no guarantee. And this is a fascist state. You will not be offered a bond while sorting things out. You will find yourself thrown in prison and you will be staying there for quite a long time."

I stared at her. She stared back for a long moment, lit the pipe, took a puff, coughed and handed it to me.

"I would implore you to get that notion out of your head right this very second. It's dangerous enough just indulging in the sport."

I nodded and took a hit. Anne's words of warning had soon evaporated into fanciful dreams. Eventually we were back to staring into each other's eyes.

"My little Abyssinian delight," I said

Anne laughed.

"God, I love the characters that drift through this place."

"I love this place, period."

"It's simply wonderful, isn't it?"

"I don't want to ever leave." I brushed Anne's dark hair over one ear and kissed her. "I don't want to leave you."

"Oh, you wildly romantic young man, you. Do you really have any idea what you want?"

"I told you. To be in this magical place…And to be with you."

Anne placed a hand to my cheek.

"Paul. You've no idea where this is headed. You can't possibly know. You're simply too young."

I shrugged.

"Who does know?"

"Ah, becoming a veritable sage as I watch."

I shrugged again.

"I'm learning…You know, when I left the States, the world seemed so terribly complicated to me. Wars, careers, politics. All this stuff I could not foresee or control. Now, here with you, I begin to see it's really simple."

I rubbed my nose to hers.

"Someone to love. A happy place to live. Some wine and good food and a few good friends."

"Yes, and I'm trying very hard not to screw that up," she said.

"Why? You think I would?"

"Let's just say I have a wary eye out here."

I took her head in my hands.

"I love this face." I kissed her. "It makes me feel very happy and content…And safe somehow."

Anne let me kiss her but pushed back when I tried to mount her.

"Not like a bloody bull, Paul. Please…take your time."

I flushed with embarrassment but Anne comforted me with kisses and was soon leading me to her bedroom. In the candlelit darkness, she pulled back her side of the bed and started to undress. I did the same and found her waiting for me under the covers.

"Hmmmm. So wonderfully warm against the cool sheets."

"As are you, dear Paul."

I still very much wanted to mount her but Anne held me back, touching me, having me touch her and signaling when I had done so in the right place and in the right way. She put her lips to me, inspiring me to put my lips to her and she smelled strangely of the sea down there. I had dreams of seahorses in the deep while tasting her pungent flesh.

Finally, she came and encouraged me to mount her and it was over in less than a minute. She caressed me and kissed me and held me tight.

"Oh, you bloody young bull you." She pulled her face back to look at me. "But you're learning. Hmm. You're learning wonderfully."

I smiled and kissed her lips gently.

"Thank you."

"For what?" she said.

"For teaching me."

"Hmm. You are a good learner. A very good learner."

I smiled.

"I still like the finish line."

Anne laughed and laughed.

We made love again that night and again in the morning and by the time we had finished with eating breakfast, I was ready for more and a nap. Anne accepted my kisses from the kitchen sink and then held me back.

"Time for chores, my dear."

"Oh, darn."

'Hmm. Your laundry?"

"Oh, sure."

She pointed.

"You know how to use a washer and dryer, I presume?"

"Marginally. It'll come back to me."

"I suspect it will."

By the time I had the laundry going, Anne was working out in the garden. She had on a sundress and a big straw hat. I joined her and helped with pulling weeds. The day was dry and still and filled with the sound of insects.

When the sun became too hot on our backs, Anne plucked a handful of tomatoes and led me back inside.

"Some pasta and homemade sauce for lunch perhaps?"

"That sounds lovely."

I kissed her.

"What else do you have to do today?"

"I should be going into town for some supplies, but it's not entirely necessary."

"I'll go with you."

"If you'd like."

"Sure. I'd go anywhere with you…"

Our kiss was interrupted by the sound of a motor scooter out in front. Anne looked that way and back at me.

"Peter," she said.

We heard voices and laughter coming in through the front door. Anne went out to investigate. I followed as far as the passageway and found Peter and two of his friends already making themselves at home in the living room.

"Oh ho!" Peter said. "Look at the tomatoes on that doll."

Anne dismissed him with a wave of her hand and returned to the kitchen. Peter followed her.

"So, were we going into town then?" he said, brushing by me.

"I was just telling Paul. I'm not entirely sure it's necessary today. Perhaps I'll wait until the cupboards are bare."

The other two men had drifted into the kitchen.

"Oh, Barret and Phillip, this is *Paul*," Peter said with a smile.

I shook their hands. Barret looked English with his pale skin, gray eyes and dark ringlets. Phillip was a suave looking Spaniard. With all of them being older, there was that sense of the dominant bucks hovering around Anne again and blocking out the young male. I went to sit in the living room and listened to the sound of their banter and laughter. When they came out from the kitchen, Anne took a seat next to me. The other men settled around the room with big smiles.

"Oobly boobly then," Peter said.

"Oh, you're incorrigible. I'll definitely not be going to town after that."

Peter already had his hash out and was filling a bowl.

"We'll dream we went," he said.

The pipe started around the room with everyone coughing. Laughter followed and the usually silly banter.

"Nice shirt," Peter said to me.

"A flute playing Kenyan came down the beach last night, selling them," Anne said. "Nice fellow. He christened Paul, raja blue daddy."

"Ha! Great name."

Everyone sat there staring at me.

"So where does raja blue daddy hail from?" Peter said.

"It's been so long, I've nearly forgotten."

"A man of the world."

There were more smiles.

"So, that trip into town," Peter said to Anne.

"Oh you bastard," she said, laughing.

"No. You can ride on the back with Phillip. I'll take Barret."

Peter looked at me with a smile.

"You can run along behind and get some exercise."

From the corner of my eye, I saw that Anne had frowned at him.

As if tired of his game, Peter collapsed backwards in his chair with arms out and his face facing the ceiling.

"God, it's all in a dream, isn't it? Right now, a car's honking in Manhattan, a Shudra's threshing wheat in Bengal, a fisherman's casting his nets in Samos, a snow leopard's stalking its prey in the Himalayas..."

"The green dolphins of Corinth are frolicking over sunken treasures," Barret said.

"A ship horn is calling in Istanbul," Phillip said.

They looked at Anne.

"The sea is breaking whitely along the shores of Madagascar," she said.

They looked at me.

"A star is twinkling above the moons of Orion."

Peter pretended to gasp.

"Not fair. You've left Earth. You've left the galaxy."

"I left the galaxy a long, long time ago."

Anne snickered. Peter smiled.

"A dhow is rowing home in the dusky lights of old Hong Kong."

The game went around the room several more times. Tiring of it, and wanting a drink, I said, "Francisco is mixing daiquiris on the fine, white sands of Formentera."

"Ha!" Peter said. "The man's a lush!"

"No, just thirsty all of a sudden."

"Well, anyone else up for a drink?"

"Oh, let's have lunch," Anne said.

She was on her feet and off to the kitchen with the other three men quickly on her heels. I went out and sat in the shade of the veranda. Their voices and laughter echoed out into the arid afternoon. Sometime later, Anne came out and kissed my forehead.

"Don't make too much of it."

I looked up at her.

"I don't."

She kissed my lips and tasted of fried garlic and tomatoes.

"Come join us."

"Why? To compete?"

"Oh stop. You're a man. You should know these games."

"I do, and I'm not particularly fond of them."

Anne looked at me caringly.

"And that's why you're in my bed and not them."

I nodded. She kissed me on the lips again and left.

Soon, I was listening to more laughter. The game was for me to go in and assert myself. To share little intimacies with Anne that would corral her off from the other bucks and mark my territory but I had no interest in that. If we were only animals, then I was something else.

Eventually, Anne came to retrieve me and the five of us sat down to a meal of pasta with sausages, a pepper, red onion and goat cheese salad and a loaf of bread. The meal was followed by another bowl of hashish and more entreaties for Anne to join the three men on an adventure into San Francisco.

It was midafternoon before Anne was finally able to chase them off. As she waved goodbye from the shade of her veranda, they waved back and headed off on their two scooters, laughing away and calling out in the arid heat.

Once they had disappeared around the bend of the narrow, sandy trail, Anne put a hand to my back and searched my eyes.

"I'm sorry," she said.

"No need for apologies."

"Okay. That's good. But please don't ever discount the things I share from my heart."

"All right."

"Honestly. All these years and I just assumed that all men liked to play these games."

"Not this one."

"So…consider me enlightened."

She stood on her tippy toes and kissed me.

"Come. Let me reassure you of your place in my heart."

Soon, her lips were tasting the salt of my belly and descending down to where dolphins swam with Corinthian treasures. A breeze had blown up from the sea and it stirred in the curtains as Anne made my wounded heart feel whole again.

Thirteen

Anne and I were sitting under her front arbor the following afternoon, she reading her Durrell and me a tale about the road, when we heard a voice call out "Hey ho!" and looked up to find Stewart dashing out from the olive grove and across the intervening, sundrenched space, his head and leather hat bowed against the heat.

"Greetings, sir," I said as he walked up.

He peeked at the cover of my tome.

"*The Road to Oxiana*. Any good."

"Yes, actually. Quite good. The British have perfected the art of turning otherwise mundane adventures into ribald tales."

Anne kicked me. Stewart laughed.

"Still laboring over that Durrell novel, I see," he said to her.

"Suffering, if you must know."

"I didn't want to be the one to say it."

I laughed. Stewart reached for our chilled bottle of wine.

"Albarino. Hmm. Any good?"

"Delightful," Anne said.

She stared.

"So, were you going to offer me a glass?"

"I'd hate to make you suffer."

"This is becoming quite a contest."

"Not really. It's my wine…Oh, did you really want some?"

"Does the president have a long nose and beady eyes?"

Anne laughed.

"I'll not get into your domestic political affairs, but I *will* get you a glass."

"Splendid," he said.

"So what's up?" I said as Anne went off to the kitchen.

"I'm heading home."

"Oh, then we definitely must have a parting toast," Anne called out over her shoulder.

"Right now?" I said to Stewart.

"Yeah. Whenever I can catch a boat out."

"Hell, sorry to see you go. What's the rush?"

"Flight goes out from Madrid in three days. Time to…"

Anne had returned with the glass and poured it full of the chilled wine. Stewart winked at me secretively. Madrid. Yeah, there it was again.

"You were saying?" Anne asked in passing the glass.

"Oh, just saying it's time to get ready for the fall semester. Unless of course you'll take me in."

"Not on your life. I've already one feral cat lying about here emptying my cupboards."

Anne smiled at me and kissed my hand.

"Your fault. You've spoiled him with modern plumbing," Stewart said.

The three of us stared, smiling.

"I suppose we should walk him over to the harbor," I said.

"And that we'll do," Anne said.

"Fantastic. I'll treat you to a meal before I go."

"Oh, thanks but we've already had lunch," Anne said.

"But we'll gladly drink in your honor."

"Splendid." He sipped at the chilled wine. "Hmm, damned good, this Albarino."

Stewart was still playing Hemingway. I pictured him doing so as the political activist on campus.

'Good god, old man. That's no way to carry a bloody protest sign. This isn't bridge. It's bloody war. Show some pluck. Courage and grace in the face of death. No room for the goddamned faint of heart here. They'll only remember the good ones when it's all over.'

I smiled at Stewart, wondering if he could read my thoughts.

"More Albarino?" I said when he had tossed back the rest of his glass.

"God, yes," he said. "Great wine. One of the good ones."

I laughed.

A short while later, Anne took the empty glasses out to the kitchen and we started across the island together on foot, avoiding the heat of the day as best we could through one shady grove after another. On the windward coast, we sat sipping wine and talking of life late into the afternoon. As the last fisherman was preparing to depart for Ibiza, we walked Stewart down to the dock. He gave us both a hug before climbing onboard.

"It's been real, brother."

"Likewise," I said.

"Do try to be civilized about your revolution," Anne said.

"Bloody English. Never could quite wean yourselves of the crown."

"It's tradition. We're terribly fond of it."

Stewart laughed.

"And trust me. Those bastards are bloody fond of you being fond of it."

"Oh, off with you."

We waved a final goodbye to Stewart as the skiff pulled away. The distant lights of Ibiza were twinkling across the darkening sea.

On our way back, I found myself overrun with melancholy. I'd nearly forgotten the original cause of my journey. And Eva.

"How about a drink at Francisco's?" I said as we neared Anne's place.

"If you promise only one."

"Only one."

She scoffed.

"Not likely. One daiquiri has a way of turning into two and three."

"It's the pitcher," I said.

Anne smiled.

"Very well, but only one."

I nodded obediently.

"All right. Let me freshen up before we go."

Anne used the bathroom, then tidied up around the kitchen a bit while I did the same and we were off. The groves were thick with dusk as we passed through them, the stone walls guarded by iridescent blue-green Pitiusan lizards, taking in the last heat of the day. As always, Metellus and his legions seemed to echo from across the ages.

As we passed through the pine grove, the orange-red campfires glowed from down at the shore. The sounds of revelry carried in the growing darkness. We stepped out onto the still warm white sand and found Mickey seated at Francisco's with his Abyssinian princess. The usual collection of vagabond souls had gathered in the last blush of a dying day.

"There be me brother in arms!" Mickey called out. "Behold the fleeting hour."

"Hey, Mickey. Barbara."

Barbara hoisted her daiquiri as we walked up.

"How're youse guys doin'?"

"Great, great."

"And to me fellow loyal subject of her majesty, the queen," Mickey said to Anne.

"I'll admit to being a subject. I don't know how loyal."

"Ah...I smell mutiny on the wind."

"Not much. I'm simply all keyed up for a revolt of some kind after discussing politics with Stewart for the past few hours."

Francisco was pouring daiquiris from his pitcher and we each took one.

"Cheers. Cheers."

With a good, long draught, I gazed out over the shore and grew lost in the magic of the moment, only vaguely aware of Anne conversing with Barbara and the general revelry. As a meerkat that had lost its tribe, only to be accepted into a new one, I felt enormously grateful right then to have found a home.

"So what be your plans, mate?" Mickey asked.

"Stay, I hope. What about you?"

Mickey tipped his head in Barbara's direction and whispered.

"As long as she'll have me, mate, I remain her faithful liege."

I chuckled. When you fleshed it out, the two of us weren't all that different. I had one more hand. Mickey wore a bit a bit more of his chivalry on his sleeve.

"I'm happy for you, Mickey. Do you know that Stewart's headed back to the mainland?"

"I knew it was his intent. So he's set sail already, has he?"

"Yeah. We saw him off about an hour ago."

"A good man, the bloody bastard."

Mickey held his glass aloft and clinked it to mine, then leaned his head over and whispered.

"I still have plans...You know that bit of mischief we had discussed. Should you care to join in."

"I don't think so, Mickey. Maybe I'd like to buy some for myself?"

"On the discount for you, lad. 'Ave no doubt about it."

"Why, did you already have something lined up?"

He leaned over even closer.

"On the tide tonight, sir. They'll be bringing ashore several hundred kilos of it and 'ave agreed to sell me two of them."

He leaned back with a smile.

"A bit of business in Barcelona and I'll be back to set up shop with me little princess here. All domestic like, we'll be."

"We'll be fine neighbors then, won't we matey?" I said in a pirate's voice.

"That we'll be."

It had been a long day from dawn until then so Anne and I were soon saying adieu and heading back through the groves to her home.

"I absolutely must make a trip for supplies tomorrow," she said, going in through the door.

"All right. I'll go with you."

She glanced over her shoulder and disappeared into the kitchen. I sat and enjoyed her movements back and forth. Lastly, I heard Anne brushing her teeth.

"So, off to sleep?" she said, plopping down onto my lap.

We kissed. Her eyes looked dark in the candlelight.

"Teach me again," I said.

"Teach you."

"Yes. I like it a lot when you teach me."

"Oh, you're impossible."

"Am I?"

She kissed me.

"Yes. But I do like the progress you've been making."

I laughed and chased Anne into her bedroom, shedding clothes and exchanging kisses as I did.

When all our passions had been extinguished and Anne was content in her dreams, I slipped out of bed and stole away with my clothes. Curiosity led me down through the groves and back to the sea. The moon was out and danced on the glassy waters through the trees.

I had neared the sand and was about to step out into plain sight when I heard the sound of oars hitting the water. I pulled back among the pines and watched two men run a sizeable skiff aground to the south of me. They jumped out and pulled the boat up out of the tide. Four other men came out of the pine grove to meet them. Waves slapped at the stern of the boat as they whispered among themselves. Their exchange of money complete, each man from shore hoisted a burlap sack over his shoulder and disappeared among the trees. The other two men shoved the skiff back into the tide and jumped in. I stayed well-hidden and watched the men row away from shore.

A quarter mile out to sea, the engine came to life and the boat raced off towards the south, I assumed back to Algeria. It was only a hundred and fifty miles away and far closer than the coast of Morocco. With a couple of jerry cans, a good motor and a bit of providence, you could make the trip in six hours.

I watched until the noise of the motor had faded to nothing and headed back to Anne's place through the grove. She stirred when I crawled back into bed and reached out with one hand.

"Where were you? I got up to use the bathroom and saw you were gone."

"I went for a walk."

She rolled over.

"Where?"

I considered lying, if only to avoid any unnecessary friction but decided to tell it straight. Anne's mood darkened measurably as I explained about the smugglers.

"Please tell me again that you're not going to involve yourself."

"I wouldn't mind buying some for myself. But smuggling? No."

"You promise?"

I nodded.

"I know how you feel about it."

"But how do you feel about it?"

"I already told Mickey. I don't want to get involved."

She stared at me for a long moment before giving me a kiss and turning back over on her side.

In the morning, after we had bathed and eaten, Anne and I headed off through the groves to San Francisco. While she took care of her business, I hid from the hot sun inside a shady café. We had lunch there once Anne was done with her errands and headed back across the island with the day still hot.

"A swim?" I said, back at Anne's place.

"Yes. Sounds lovely."

We gathered together a picnic basket with a bottle of chilled wine, some fruit and cheese, an umbrella and two beach towels and headed off through the groves. At the shore, we noticed Barbara sitting at Francisco's bar, sans Mickey. We said hello in passing and learned that he had gone off to Barcelona, perhaps unawares in his absence that his Abyssinian princess was being pursued by a pack of new suitors.

Anne and I walked some distance down the shore and made camp. I dug out the sand so that we had something of a backrest beneath our towels and we had a swim before settling there under our umbrella. The sea immediately along the shore was as crystal-clear as a backyard swimming pool, the sand white, the sky cerulean and the pines dark-green behind us. The pines sighed in the heat of the day and the sea swished gently at our feet. We sipped our wine and talked, enjoying it all.

Anne had all sorts of new questions about my life and how I had gotten there and I told her everything I could, leaving out the many women involved. Anne explained that her father had been killed in the war and her mother had passed away young from cancer, which had left Anne with both a sizable trust and pension. She was set for life, as long as she didn't blow it.

A young man could be forgiven for thinking, well, let's not blow this, either.

At the end of the day, we stopped at Francisco's and learned that Apollo 11 was scheduled to land on the moon in several hours.

"Jesus. I'd completely forgotten," I said to Anne.

"We having a big moon landing party here tonight," Francisco said. "¿It's very good, si?"

"It's a wonderful idea," Anne said. "Shall we go freshen up then and hurry back?" she said to me.

"Yes, let's do."

We made our way back to her place, showered, shared a light meal and returned to the beach with Anne's binoculars and a blanket. A sizable crowd had already gathered on the beach and was all abuzz. We made ourselves comfortable among the many blankets spread out in the fine white sand.

In honor of the event, Francisco had turned off the music and turned on a transistor radio to the raw NASA feed. The landing craft was then making its way down to the lunar surface. We heard the transmission crackle each time the astronauts said something to Houston and each time Houston answered back. Back and forth it went with the orbiter growing ever closer. At twilight, the moon rose in the deep blue sky to great cheers. For however many thousands of years, that mysterious orb had stirred the imaginations of mankind and now one of us was about to land on it for the first time. Anne and I took turns staring up at the moon through her binoculars.

"Hey, I think I see them," I said to much laughter.

The atmosphere grew tense as the transmissions suggested the lander had overshot its target and might run out of fuel. There was silence for the better part of a minute. Then we heard the transmission crackle again and the words.

"Houston. Tranquility Base here. The eagle has landed."

From all nationalities, wild cheers erupted. The first man had touched down on that uncertain soil. Reports came in from all over the world – Times Square to Hong Kong, the dusty streets of Texas to monks in Katmandu – the sound and impressions of people in distant lands, everyone on earth in that moment seeming as one.

The sense of awe followed Anne and I home to her place that evening and remained with me over the ensuing days. There was news of the astronauts returning home and being feted with parades and visits to the president. Then life on the island seemed to have settled back into its usual routine.

One afternoon, I noticed Barbara flirting with this wild French rogue and scion of a family fortune. He called himself an artist. What he no doubt represented to Barbara was the sweet life.

The next day, the two of them were not to be found. Mickey returned the following afternoon, having been gone for a little over week. I was at Francisco's trying to stay cool in the heat of the day and enjoying a daiquiri when he reappeared.

Mickey strutted up triumphantly, looking for all the world like a gold miner fresh into town after a big strike. He had bathed and shaved. His clothes were pressed and cleaned. There was a new air about him.

"Mickey," I said. "How is our ancient mariner?"

"Mate, me sails be trimmed like never before."

He searched the bar and beach towels scattered around the sand.

"All set to indulge my little princess," he said. "So where be she?"

I shrugged. I didn't have the heart to tell him.

Francisco poured Mickey a daiquiri without asking. Mickey looked from face to face and the message slowly sunk in.

"So, gone on to distant shores, 'as she?"

I shrugged and nodded. The air seemed to go out of him. Several of those nearest to Mickey offered him a reassuring pat on the shoulder.

"I won't ask to where or under what circumstances 'Twould only add to my grief."

"I'm sorry, Mickey," I said.

Mickey looked down and shook his head. After a moment, his eyes came up and looked at me.

"Plucked me heart and stolen it away, she has. But 'tis the way of life. And there now. I've had me moment of grief. Let's all 'ave a round in her honor."

"Francisco!" he called out. "A round of drinks on me."

A minute later, with glasses held high, we bid a somber farewell to the Abyssinian princess.

Mickey hung around for two more days, just long enough to bag a few more kilos of hashish and was off again. He had tried one more time to convince me to join his enterprise but I was quite content to live my simple life with Anne.

"You can be sure of me return, mate," Mickey said before shoving off. "And if you see my little princess, tell her that all is forgiven."

"I will."

The skiff motored off, broke the waves outside the harbor and was soon lost beyond the horizon. I walked back to Anne's place through the olive groves, wondering if I would ever see him again.

The days continued to drift along, the rest of the world far away and mostly forgotten. Like a cat, I lounged about Anne's house, purring with her affections and otherwise doing enough chores to keep from being thrown out. Occasionally, the feral part of me grew restless and I would stay out at night, even intriguing with other women, but drawn to sit about the campfires with my own generation more than anything, sharing stories and singing songs and recalling the simpler days gone by, before the war had cast its shadow over the world.

The days turned to weeks and the weeks into a month. Having called the consulate from San Francisco one day, I knew my passport was waiting for me and had been advised that it would be best if I returned to retrieve it promptly. My temporary visa had expired and there was no telling what the Spanish authorities would do, if they became aware of the situation. Quite possibly lock me up. I assured the consulate that I would be back soon, though I had no real interest in abandoning that carefree life and sailing off to Barcelona.

One night, when I had arrived home alone very late from Francisco's, Anne turned over in bed and stared at me.

"What do I represent to you, Paul?"

I stared.

"You have no idea, do you?"

She shook her head slowly.

"I had asked you at the very beginning, what do you want from me? You had no answer then and you have no answer now."

I stared.

"Oh Paul. I can't do this any longer."

I sighed and hung my head. Anne reached out a hand and made me sit on the bed.

"Paul, I understand and don't fault you. You're young and can see no end to the time at hand, but I'm of that age when you start to think, well, how will things be in ten or twenty years from now? You find yourself wanting to know that someone will be there through thick and thin, until the very end."

She shook my hand.

"I know there are no guarantees, but I also know how this will play out. One day you'll grow bored and move on, leaving me with all these sweet moments I'll come to regret..."

I started to interject but Anne stopped me.

"No. Please accept my feelings. I want you to leave."

Seeing me crestfallen, she reached out a hand.

"Not today. Perhaps not even soon but let's agree. Someday. We must go our separate ways."

"But I can be better. I love you. I don't want to go away."

Anne stared, looking more chagrined by my words than comforted.

"What?" I said.

"What, Paul? Do you realize it's the first time you've ever uttered those words?"

I shrugged.

"I've been hurt too."

"Have you now?"

I nodded.

"Then why haven't you ever spoken about it?"

"I don't know. I guess I just feel safer hiding things away."

Anne sighed.

"Please don't make me go."

She sighed even more deeply now.

"It would help if I knew something about you."

"All right."

"All right," she said, waiting.

Haltingly, I went forward, explaining how I had gotten to Europe but leaving out any mention of Anastasia and Heidi. By the end, Anne was wiping at tears.

"Oh dear, sorry, but don't you see? Every woman wants to be loved in that way, this one included."

"But I do love you in that way."

"Hmm." Anne reached for a box of tissues and dealt with her sniffles. "Well, you've certainly not said a word to me about it."

"I'm sorry, but I really do."

Anne allowed me to kiss her lips but quickly pulled away.

"I'm willing to see how things go. That's all I can say. I trust that's all right."

I nodded and silently accepted my new probationary status.

Fourteen

Several days later, I sat in the shade of Francisco's bar, sipping the usual daiquiri while being transported by the many lovely shades of blue and white that surrounded me. I found the way the turquoise sea turned a dark blue a hundred yards offshore especially enchanting.

The sea swished. The pines whispered. It was a perfectly lovely day but my thoughts were troubled. Things had never been quite the same between Anne and I since our confrontation.

It occurred to me that romances were like chess matches, the end assured long before the loser was willing to acknowledge defeat. You forged ahead, not knowing how many moves were left in the game, but damned well sure they were finite. I had learned that a couple of orgasms could solve a lot of problems — just about anything, really — and in general employed that salve for whatever ailed us, but the matter of my reduced status always bled back through the ensuing silences.

Adding to my troubled state of mind that day, Peter and his friends had been over at Anne's place the previous night, being their usual jackasses, and though she was always quick to offer a reassuring hand, in my darkest moments, I imagined her delighting in my discomfort. The two of us had plans for a trip over to Barcelona in a few days, she on business, me in order to retrieve my passport and that's where things presently stood.

The last time Mickey had returned to the island, I had purchased several ounces of hashish from him and had been selling if off gram by gram to passing tourists. That commerce had allowed me to salt away a chunk of money, a fallback position if Anne did finally run me off.

The stash itself was stored in a canning jar at the base of one of the stone walls, off at the far end of the pine grove, and if anyone asked when Anne was around, I played dumb. If she wasn't around, I made the deal. Either way, I always kept a bit of hashish in my pocket for pleasure. Everyone on the island did. It was as ubiquitous as chewing gum.

I had been sitting there for the better part of the afternoon, sorting through these thoughts, and was just thinking to take a final dip in the sea before heading home when Mickey appeared out of the pine grove.

"You're back," I said.

"Yes, and not for tea and nattering, mate. I plan to shove off on the tide and recommend you do the same."

"Why? What the hell for?"

"The bloody Guarda. They're everywhere and on the march."

I looked around us.

"Everywhere?"

"Around the port on Ibiza for now but they're amassing and appear to have a Roman like invasion in mind."

"For Formentera?"

He nodded.

"Why? You think they're on to the smuggling?"

"What else, mate? There be little reason otherwise for their presence."

I considered the news and shrugged.

"So why the delay? Why wouldn't they come right away?"

"I can see you've no experience with marshalling an expeditionary force."

"You think they're waiting for darkness."

"That be when all the mischief takes place."

"So why did you come back?"

"To warn you, mate. It's all for one and one for all."

I smiled.

"You're a hell of a friend, Mickey. Have a daiquiri."

"One and we're off, agreed?"

"Hell, I can't just up and leave Anne without a word. She's over in San Francisco today."

"Then I suggest we make our way over to the windward side and settle in at the Conch Café. Should the invasion occur, we'll likely have a bloody front row seat and be none the worse for watching. And it's an easy slip from there up to the harbor and safety."

"I'm awfully comfortable sitting right here in the shade."

"If you like shade, mate, the dungeon has plenty to spare."

I shrugged.

"All right. I guess I can be just as comfortable over at the Conch."

I paid up my tab and started off through the pine grove with Mickey. The late summer day was thick with heat and insects.

It time, the cheery blue colors of the opposite coast came into view. At the Conch, I switched to cold beer and listened to Mickey recount his latest adventures. He had been up the coast as far as Italy, exploring supply routes, with plans of expanding into a major smuggling operation. The day slowly faded to dusk with the sound of lanyards clanging nearby.

I was about to thank Mickey for the warning and head back to Anne's place when the prow of a boat appeared over the horizon. Then another one appeared, and another one, until we had an entire flotilla of patrol boats churning towards us.

"Christ, I'd better go warn Anne," I said, getting up.

Mickey grabbed my arm.

"No, mate. They'll sweep up every loose thing in their path."

"Screw it. I'm not going to leave her unawares."

Mickey gripped my arm more firmly.

"I'm telling you, mate. She'll be fine in her little cottage. Their focus be on that little spit of shoreline south of Francisco's. If anything, give them ample distance and follow in their wake."

We both watched as the first boat arrived to the docks. Another boat quickly followed, and another one. A small army of soldiers had piled out and were unloading motorbikes and weapons. Two officers were busy directing the landing. Mickey and I sat there with our beers frozen in our hands.

As soon as the invasion had swept up the dock and disappeared behind us, I jumped to my feet.

"Wait," Mickey said again.

"No, I've got to go find Anne."

"I'm telling you, mate. She'll be fine. My money's on them setting up shop in the pine grove and waiting for the smugglers to row ashore."

I watched the invasion sweep off across the island from a back window, feeling cowardly for waiting but knowing that Mickey was right. Best to let the soldiers get a good distance out ahead before I followed.

With all of them gone out of sight, I could no longer restrain myself and headed for the front door. Mickey followed me outside and grabbed me by the arm again.

"I know your intentions be noble, mate, but I've a grim premonition. Let's make for Ibiza. No doubt both our names and faces be known down there."

"You don't have to go, Mickey but I've got to make sure Anne's all right."

"Fortune be with you then. I'll stay behind and secure a means of passage. If you're not back here within the hour, I'll be off with the tide."

"Fine. If you don't see me back here within the hour, get your ass to Ibiza."

I gripped him by the shoulder, stared into his eyes and dashed off into the darkening grove. Several times, I stopped to listen for sounds up ahead, then ran again. Ten minutes later, I was staring across the road at Anne's place. There were sounds of mayhem down at the shore but all was quiet around me.

I ran across the road and slipped inside. There were no signs of Anne or anyone. While I considered a course of action, I heard muffled voices outside and peeked out a window. A number of people were fleeing away from the shore in the umbrage.

I went to Anne's desk and quickly scribbled out a note. I had escaped the soldiers and was heading back to Barcelona for my passport. I would look for her every night at six around the statue of Columbus. I had come to make sure she was safe but had to go.

With the note written, I quickly gathered things into my pack.

Back out in the grove, I stumbled upon two more young couples fleeing towards the opposite shore. They were as startled by me as I was by them. Realizing we were compatriots, everyone relaxed.

"What's going on?" I said.

"Fuck, the soldiers are holding everyone at gun point down on the beach," one of the men said. "They wrecked Francisco's. Fucking everything."

"The bastards," the other man said.

I quickly described Anne.

"Do any of you know her? Did any of you see her down there?"

They shared looks and shook their heads.

"So how did you get out?"

"We had hiked down the shore exploring and saw the scene from a distance," the first guy said.

"Yeah, all of our shit is down there," the second one said.

"What do you think?" one of the women said. "Should we go back for it?"

"Probably not. Not tonight anyway. They're looking for smugglers and the boat doesn't come in until late so they'll probably hold everyone until at least morning."

The men cursed.

"So what are you going to do?" the first guy asked me.

The five of us searched each other's eyes in the darkness.

"I'm heading back to The Conch. A friend of mine is trying to arrange a boat out tonight."

"Do you think you can carry us too?"

"I don't know if we can get everyone onboard but we can try. Money can buy anything, even on this island. If nothing else, you can hide out until morning and see about finding your own boat."

Just then we heard something crack in the brush and saw searchlights coming our way through the pine grove. Cursing, we all turned and ran. A couple of times the women stopped to catch their breath and the men fell back with them. I did not stop until I reached the far side of the island. Mickey was nowhere in sight.

"Wait inside the Conch Café," I said when they caught up with me. "I'm going to look for my friend. If I don't come back, we couldn't carry you."

They stared.

"Look, I don't know what else to say. Just act like you're tourists and the soldiers will probably ignore you."

I left them going into The Conch. One of the men stopped and watched me disappear down the street. On the other end of Es Caló, I ran into Mickey.

"What's the plan?"

"I was unable to rouse a soul here so it's on to Es Pujols, mate. She's home to most of the fishing boats."

"All right. Let's go."

I explained the rest as we moved up the coast. Half an hour later, we came to the outskirts of the sleeping village and moved cautiously down to the sea. Fishing boats rocked quietly on the dark water.

"Looks like we'll be waiting until dawn," Mickey said.

We made ourselves comfortable in the lee of a seawall and settled in for the night. Mickey had a flask of brandy so we passed that back and forth from time to time. Between the brandy and the adrenalin slowly wearing off, we eventually grew weary and found sleep.

Mickey awakened first and gently shook me. It was still before dawn. We sat there in the cold, watching the sky slowly brighten on the eastern horizon. Then the first fishermen came down the streets from the town and threw his gear onboard a skiff. Mickey went down to speak with him. A minute later, Mickey waved me on.

"He wants two thousand pesetas," Mickey whispered. "Fears the Guarda more than we do."

"Fine."

We each gave him a thousand pesetas.

The fisherman started the motor.

"Vaminos," he said.

We climbed in and lay low in the hull until we were well out to sea. The sky to the east had turned blood red by then. The old man had told us he would not risk the harbor and instead slipped into a cove south of town. Mickey and I jumped out into knee deep water. The old man acknowledged our thanks with a wave and turned the boat back out to sea.

We waded into shore, started up the steep cliffs and later came to be standing on a promontory overlooking the town. Life was beginning to stir in the streets below us. Continuing down towards the waterfront, we passed an old woman sweeping the street out in front of her shop. A man went by on a bicycle with fresh bread. We walked on until the harbor came into view. It was still bristling with troops.

There was nothing to do but settle into a bar and wait. We felt reasonably safe doing that. What happened when we attempted to board a ferry to Barcelona was another matter.

The overnight ferry pulled into port about an hour after sunrise. By then, Mickey and I had eaten breakfast and were sipping coffee. The patent leathers milled around the dock as everyone disembarked. We watched them ask to see this or that person's papers before moving on.

"I say we chance it now," Mickey said when it was time to board the now outgoing ferry.

I glanced at him, knowing there were two basic choices. Sit tight and wait them out, or leave on the tide. I also knew that Anne would have to pass through Ibiza on her way to Barcelona so I was inclined to wait. That said, given the mischief on Formentera, it was possible she might delay her trip for days and the Guarda might remain here on patrol for weeks. Finally, there was the simple fact that if Mickey left without me, I would be all alone on Ibiza and was not keen on that idea.

"All right, let's go," I said.

"Right you are, mate. Wait for the crowd, slip aboard and Bob's your uncle. Just one thing, though."

"What?"

"We're not boarding in this gear."

I was still wearing my raja blue daddy shirt. Mickey was still Errol Flynn.

"Yeah, you're probably right about that."

"Right as right, mate. Let's 'ave bottoms up and be off for a new wardrobe."

In a shop well back from the waterfront, he bought a striped peasant shirt. I changed into mine and stuffed the other shirts into my backpack. Then we went down to buy two tickets. With people boarding the ferry, Mickey and I joined the line in separate places and inched forward under the glowering eyes of the Guarda. I passed by one of them with my heart beat wildly. It wasn't until I had cleared the gangway and was safely onboard that my heart finally stilled.

"We're on our way, mate," Mickey said when he found me.

"Those bastards," I said. "They make you feel like the inquisition."

"That's their job in life."

We went to the rail. I searched the waterfront for any sign of Anne. Mickey pulled out his flask of brandy.

"This should keep us right."

"Yeah. I'll wait until later," I said.

"She'll show up in Barcelona," Mickey said with a pat on my back.

Once the ferry was at sea, we settled into our chairs. Mickey went on bantering about his recent adventures. I kept thinking of Anne.

We arrived back to Barcelona around six and went to the sailor bar where we had first met. There was no need to check the plaza that evening. Mickey and I closed the bars and shared a room for the night.

In the morning, Mickey went off to take care of business. I bathed before abandoning the room and made my way to the consulate. With passport in hand, I took a bus north along the coast. We passed the exclusive beach clubs with their carved wooden doors open to the sea. I saw the rows of brightly colored umbrellas in the sun and thought of Heidi, which turned my thoughts back towards Anne. Anastasia too. And Eva. All these beautiful women. And here I was all alone again.

At the public beach, I got off and went looking for a gypsy in knee high leather boots. I wasn't sure what I planned to do if I ever found the bastard who had robbed me but figured to play that by ear. The gypsies were all down by the mouth of the flood channel, bathing in the public showers. I cursed the bastards. There was no sign of my boots, or my camera.

At six, I went to wait for Anne at the plaza. Mickey showed up and waited with me. After an hour or so, we went back to our favorite bar.

The next day passed in much the same manner. I cursed myself for having left Anne behind. It had been cowardly of me to abandon her.

"Give it up, mate," Mickey said when Anne failed to show on that second night. "Why don't we rum it down to Marrakesh."

"No. She'll come. If not, I'm heading back."

"The best then, mate. Time for me to set sail."

"I'll see you, Mickey. You take care."

"The same to you, mate. You take this then."

He furtively handed me what looked to be an entire ounce of hashish.

"Wow. Thanks, Mickey."

"To my brother in arms."

I gave him a hug and watched him head back in among the docks.

When Anne failed to show on the third night, I took the overnight ferry back to Ibiza. On Ibiza, I sat in the same bar with the windows open to the harbor, waiting for the fishermen to return with their morning catch. When they did, I arranged passage to Formentera for later that morning.

The ride across the seas was filled with anticipation. I arrived to Anne's place and found it boarded up. A note on the door said she had gone off to England for a month. That hurt. Apparently she hadn't even bothered with trying to find me before leaving.

Down at the shore, I found Francisco's bar gone and the beach mostly abandoned. A wonderful era had come to an end.

I hurried back to Ibiza and boarded the next ferry to Barcelona. That night, I drank to get drunk and tried to kick the feelings. After all I had been through, how could I be all alone again? In that moment, it seemed as if things would always be that way for me in this world.

With a little over four hundred dollars to my name and the chunk of hash Mickey had given me, I rented a room and spent two days weighing my options. There was a thought to head home, but that sounded too much like defeat. Better to resume my search for Eva's uncle. And there I was, back to my original quest.

Late that afternoon, I came to be seated on a bench beneath the shade of some trees in the Plaça de Catalunya, watching people go by. In the fading light, an old pensioner walked out onto the central plaza, bearing himself along with a cane. He looked quite dignified, despite his rumpled suit and bent frame.

He had a bag of popcorn and began tossing it onto the plaza tiles. Pigeons quickly swooped in and overcame him. They were at his feet and hands and attempting to roost anywhere that space would allow on his rumpled suit. In short order, there were so many beating wings attached to him, I thought surely he would take flight. Amidst the beating wings, the arms of the old man could be seen, urgently trying to rid themselves of the remaining popcorn.

I laughed. Well, there I was in sixty years, an old man with a cane and popcorn and my pigeons, while some young man sat off to the side, having a good laugh at my infirmities.

A great restlessness overtook me suddenly and I got up to leave. I knew it would be best to make a fresh start of it in the morning but I had to move on.

Half an hour later, I was headed north up the coast from Barcelona. A young man from France gave me a lift and it was pleasant to be speaking in French again. I was truly tired of everything Spanish.

Ten miles north of the city, we came along the shore with the white-capped sea off to our right in the late afternoon wind and the wild beauty of it moved my heart. The colors. The movement. That glimpse of eternity at dusk.

A few miles farther ahead, the road turned inland and we passed through a small village. The road then came back along the sea and the magic was gone in the growing darkness. We passed a sign that said we were entering France.

Fifteen

My ride turned off at Narbonne and west towards Toulouse. There at the side of the road in the gathering gloom, I checked my map. It was still roughly a hundred miles up ahead to where the highway split at Nimes. One route would take me north and up over the Alps, the other east along the coast towards Marseille and Cinque Terra.

I put that concern off until tomorrow and walked into town for dinner. Afterward, armed with a bottle of wine, a chunk of gouda and a loaf of bread for the road, I headed back to where a park bordered the highway and coast. My thought was to camp on the beach but the terrain quickly grew hilly and rugged so I contented myself with a place under some trees and settled in for the night. The usual debate over my past and plans for the future went on in my head. I drank a bit of the wine and fell asleep late in the darkness.

In the morning, I had a bit of the cheese and bread and wine for breakfast, cleaned up as best I could and marched back out to the highway. The rides came hard that day. Sometime in the early afternoon, a farmer picked me up in Gallargues-le-

Montueux and dropped me off in Bernis, just east of Nimes. It was a drab place of small industry. The highway split five miles farther up ahead.

I had been standing there for nearly half an hour and was considering whether or not to march up to that split in the highway when a BMW pulled to the side of the road. I hesitated, not sure it had stopped for me until the driver honked. I ran up and found a woman in her thirties smiling through the window. She waved for me to get in.

"Merci," I said, placing my backpack on the back seat.

"De rien," she said.

"Paul," I said, climbing in front and getting settled.

"Jean. Enchanté."

I smiled.

"Enchanté."

Jean looked into the rearview mirror and pulled back onto the highway. I stole repeated glances at her as we motored along. She had short brown hair, lovely hazel eyes, a button nose and a ready smile. She caught me looking and smiled.

"Parlez vous Francais?"

"Oui."

She asked where I was going and I related my plans, to take the coast road through Cinque Terra and look for a man in Turin. Jean explained that she was headed up into the Alps and could drop me off very near the Mt. Blanc tunnel. From there it would only be roughly 160 kilometers to Turin, about 100 miles. It was in fact very much faster going that way and she would be happy to take me. My heart said take the coast but the prospect of being that close to Turin by the end of the day was too much to ignore. I nodded.

"Oui."

Jean smiled and turned her attention back to the highway.

"You speak the language very well," she said.

I gestured to say, com ci, com ca.

"I got an A in high school. Especially for my accent."

"It is very good. A bit provincial, but very good."

I pretended to be mortally wounded and she laughed.

"Ah, so I'm not Parisian. C'est dommage."

Jean studied me for a moment and laughed again.

"Feel free to change the music if you'd like."

She was listening to the something along the lines of Charles Aznavour. I asked if Jean knew of a rock station. She played with the dial and *I'm A Man* by the Spencer Davis Group came on.

"Oh, far out," I said and turned it up a bit.

Jean viewed my enthusiasm with a smile and asked about my generation. What had it been like growing up in America? We talked and talked and I eventually confessed to my reasons for being in Europe. Jean looked over at me several times before returning her attention to the road, her smile having grown more pensive now.

"And are you still in love with this young woman?" she asked with a glance.

I shrugged. I didn't know if I was. Looking back through the prism of Anne and Heidi and Anastasia, I no longer knew what I felt.

"I like being in love," I said.

That was, in the end, all I knew for certain. Jean studied me and reached over to touch my hand.

"Are you hungry?"

I nodded. She nodded back and pulled over to the right hand lane. We had passed the turnoff to A54 and were astride Rochefort-du-Gard. Jean exited into the little village and found a shop that sold sandwiches. She bought two, along with a bottle of wine.

"I know a nice place where we can eat outside," she said.

We returned to the highway and drove on until we were somewhere north of Bollène. Jean pulled off, drove down by the river and parked alongside a field bordered on either side by a row of poplars. The poplars ran off into the distance and were alive in the afternoon wind. Jean had a blanket in the trunk and we lay on it, eating our sandwiches and talking of life.

When I was through with my sandwich, I lay on my back and stared up at the wildly blowing poplars. Jean lay on her side, studying me. I looked over.

"Where are you going?" I asked.

"To meet my husband in Geneva."

I nodded and looked back up at the poplars.

Jean squeezed my hand.

"You are in France. You know that, yes?"

I looked back at her. Yes, I understood. It was quite normal for married people to have lovers in France but I wasn't sure how I felt about that. My instincts were to have a woman all to myself.

Jean squeezed my hand again and lay her head on my shoulder. It suddenly felt as if I was in a dream, this summer afternoon in the fields of France with a beautiful woman and the wild poplars whispering above us. I looked over at Jean. A particularly strong gust of wind stirred in the trees and we kissed.

It was nearing sunset when we finally returned to her car and the highway. Along the way, she explained that her husband owned a vineyard and she could arrange for me to have a job there, along with a place to stay. She would even provide me with a Vespa to use. If things did not work out in Turin, she welcomed me to come.

We were now winding our way up into the Alps and as we talked, I found myself trying to picture her husband and how he would feel about this arrangement. If she got me a job in his vineyard, surely he would know I was his wife's lover.

Then anxiety gripped me. Jean would soon be dropping me off in the mountains and I would be sleeping alone again out in the cold and dark. It was well past nine when she pulled into Megève and stopped in front of an inn.

"Is this where you're staying," I asked.

"No. Just wait here a minute."

She got out and disappeared inside. I worried while waiting, unwilling to spend what little funds I had on an expensive room. I assumed that was what Jean had in mind. I waited with the darkening peaks towering above me.

Jean returned a few minutes later, found a piece of paper and pen and jotted down her address and phone number.

"Our vineyard is just outside of Montpellier. Ask in town. Anyone can help you find us." She held my hand. "Please, come see me."

I nodded. She touched my face and kissed me sweetly.

"Go. The concierge is expecting you."

I got out of the car and went around to Jean's window. She kissed me again through the open window.

"I hope you find happiness," Jean said. "In either case, I will think of you, oui?"

I kissed her again and started down the road, thinking to camp in the woods but Jean pulled up beside me and rolled down the passenger window.

"No, no. Go inside."

I leaned down to look in the window. Jean waved a hand at the inn and waited until I reluctantly started that way. I assumed to greet the owner, learn how much it cost and politely decline. No doubt by then Jean would have disappeared.

An old woman greeted me warmly inside and asked me to sign the guest book. I waved a hand.

"How much is it for one night?"

"No, monsieur. Everything is already arranged. You sign, that is all."

Understanding now, I rushed back outside but Jean was gone. When I returned inside, the old woman was smiling.

"You see? Everything is already arranged."

I nodded and signed the book. She invited me to go clean up in my room. Dinner would be ready upon my return.

Fifteen minutes later, I was eating a fine stew with wine and bread and cheese. The concierge let me take what was left of the wine up to my room. I sat out on the balcony until late, drinking it and reflecting back on my journey. So many wondrous things had happened and yet there I was all alone again. The one thing I wanted, to be happily in love, was forever fleeting. I missed Jean already as I sat there.

I awakened in the morning at a bit past eight. The clean sheets felt cool and crisp in the early autumn air. Beyond the balcony, I could see grassy mountain slopes rising up steeply above me, and then craggy peaks even higher up, with those peaks still checkered in snow here and there. It was quiet save for the buzz of insects and the clang of a cow bell. It seemed as if neither the proprietor nor any of her maids were yet stirring. I pushed the sheets aside and went out to sit on the balcony. The valley cascaded far, far down to what looked like a miniature town, with many brightly colored buildings and red roofs and a tall church steeple rising above everything else.

A bit later, someone knocked at the door. I answered it and found a maid standing out in the hallway with a breakfast tray in her hands. I thanked her and took the tray out to the balcony. There were three croissants, a bowl of fresh berries and coffee. I buttered one of the croissants, lavished it with preserves, poured cream into the coffee and devoured the croissant while enjoying the scenery. A car came along the steep mountainside opposite me, moving in and out of the morning shadows. There were towering peaks very high up among the drifting white clouds and the village far, far down in the valley.

The reason for me being in Europe jumped in my heart. Six thousand miles, chasing after a woman and for what? Eva's parents had given her a choice—a man's love or the family fortune—and Eva had gone for the money. Oh well. She was not the woman for me, so none of that mattered now.

One by one, I recalled the other women. Anastasia's sheer beauty, Heidi's spunk, Ann's witty charm and Jean's sincere kindness. I saw all their faces and remembered their affections and ached for all of them one more time. My romance with Eva was nonsense in comparison.

Devouring the other croissants, I gulped down the last of the cafe au lait and closed my eyes to the morning breeze. My plan was to go on to Turin, but I could just as easily camp in the Alps for a week and return to Montpellier. Jean's offer held out the prospect of remaining in Europe indefinitely. What did I know about Eva's rich uncle? He might not even like me, or be willing to help.

Either way, I had to do something. What I had in American dollars was not enough to pay for a plane ticket back home.

Back inside the room, I showered, dressed and threw the pack over my shoulders. The proprietor said adieu on my way out of the chalet. It was a short walk out to the main road in the shade of the mountains. The Mt. Blanc tunnel was roughly ten miles away. Italy was at the end of the tunnel, and Turin a half day's journey beyond that. Best to go see. Maybe Eva's uncle was part of my destiny and there would be plenty of time to return to Montpellier and Jean if not.

The sun cleared the mountains and grew hot on my back. Now and then a car came by but no one stopped. Soon, it was midmorning, and what had seemed simple began to feel like a curse. I took off my jacket and rolled it into my sleeping bag. All the while, cars kept passing by without stopping. My flannel shirt came off next. I was down to my striped jersey by the time a tractor rig pulled to the side of the road. I ran forward with my pack and opened the door. A lean, dark haired fellow in his early thirties waved me aboard.

"Buon giorno," he said with a big white smile. "Mi chiamo Antonio. Et tu ?"

"Paulo," I said.

"Eh, parla?"

"No," I answered. "Non parlo Italiano. Parlez-vous français ?"

"Oui, bon, je parle français."

204

I was thrilled to learn that he was going through to the outskirts of Turin and explained my own plans. He told me about his brother in Brooklyn. We tried English, then Italian but returned to French. All the while, the big truck lumbered up the mountain road with cars speeding around us.

Soon, we had entered the tunnel. It went on for miles before dumping us out into a blinding sun and the arid, Italian countryside. Both Antonio and I quickly donned sunglasses.

A mile ahead, we came to a line of cars awaiting customs. I found my passport and Antonio handed it to the agent. After a quick review, he stamped it and waved us through.

The terrain had been utterly transformed from one end of the tunnel to the other, the hills now dry where they fell away from the Alps. Our slow, steady descent led us past stone houses and stone churches surrounded by dry fields, everything in varying shades of brown. There were peasants here and there in the fields and alongside the roads.

We eventually came to a vast agriculture plain, lush with crops and a sleepy agrarian peace. The green fields went on and on.

Dusk had fallen by the time we reached Turin. Antonio pulled to the side of the road, waved goodbye and pulled the truck back into traffic.

I walked several blocks and turned onto a cobblestone street. A grass promenade ran down the center of it, shrouded by elms. An old gasoline pump stood beneath the trees, with a narrow turn out for people to stop and fill up their tanks. Four old men were gathered in a circle of chairs on the grass next to the pumps. A large metal tub filled with ice sat between them, with several bottles of wine shoved into the ice. All the bottles had been opened and re-corked. Typical of old men, they were all gray haired or balding to some degree. I approached them wearing my pack.

"Ciao," one of the men said.

"Ciao. Je suis Americain," I said.

"Mais, il parle français," another man said.

The exchange seemed to amuse them. One man gestured for me to sit down and rid myself of my pack. I did both and watched as he poured me a glass of cold burgundy.

In the growing twilight, the trees stirred. Opera music poured out from a nearby window. I was suddenly aware again of being far away from home.

"Comment s'appellez vous?" one of the men asked after I drank.

"Paul."

"Paulo," he said, reverting to his native language.

There was silence, during which the men exchanged glances and looked back at me.

"Oui, Paul Fitzgerald," I added. "Mais, ma mère est Italien."

"Ah, Italiano." They liked this.

"Quelle nom?" another asked.

"Orsini."

"Orsini!!!"

In unison, they all leaned forward in their chairs.

"Guarda gente ! Lui veramente e un Italiano !"

They had all gestured with both hands in saying this.

"Eh, Orsini!" the first man said with a pat on my leg. "Quelle nom! Quelle nom!"

Having introduced ourselves, their animated conversation resumed — sometimes with me, sometimes without. I heard them mention Orsini several times. It had been a grand name back in the day, popes and princes, more ancient and illustrious than Medici, though not much more than the mark of noble peasantry by the time it had reached our branch of the family.

Encouraged to drink my wine, I did and was quickly poured another glass. The trees stirred. The occasional car came down the street.

When a woman pulled in for gas, the old man who owned the station got up to pump for her. While he did, I was able to convey my interest in finding Eva's uncle.

"Oh, si, si," one of the men said.

They all knew of him. Giuseppe, the youngest looking of them offered to lead me there.

Flush from both the wine and the prospect of finding Eva's uncle, I thanked the others and departed down a narrow backstreet with Giuseppe. Many turns followed. We came to a busy boulevard, hurried across it and turned again down a long dark lane. All the while my hopes and anticipation grew.

At last we arrived at the iron gate of a sprawling villa and Giuseppe rang the bell. A minute later, an old man came to the gate and the two men spoke in Italian. By the tone of the conversation, I knew the uncle wasn't there but Giuseppe felt obliged to explain all of it again to me in French. The uncle had indeed gone to the coast to escape the summer heat. The servant started for the house but I called him back.

"Please," I told Giuseppe. "Ask him if he knows where."

Giuseppe did. The man looked warily at me and shook his head. He was not at liberty to divulge this information. Again, he started back inside.

"No, no," I said. "Gabriele. Gabriele. La nièce est mon petit ami."

The man paused, still not convinced by the look on his face, but when Giuseppe repeated what I had said in Italian, his attitude softened.

"Eh, bene," the man said and rattled off quite a bit in Italian.

"Grazie, grazie," Giuseppe said.

The man nodded and left.

Giuseppe explained to me that the uncle had a villa in the town of Noli. If I took the main road down to Savona, it was less than ten miles up the coast from there. The servant had said to ask around. Everyone knew of the uncle.

Giuseppe asked if he could do anything else for me.

"No, no. Grazie, grazie."

We shook hands and bid farewell.

I stopped for dinner nearby, purchased a bottle of wine to warm my evening alone and followed my map to the southernmost outskirts of Turin. I had hiked for several miles when I came to an open field and some woods alongside the River Po. Having made camp beneath a windbreak of elms, I mixed a bit of hash into one of my cigarettes, smoked it, drank from the wine and dreamed of the various jobs Eva's uncle might have me do—his chauffeur, his errand boy, a big shot running his businesses.

When I wasn't thinking of that, my head was revisiting all the women I had known and loved. Anne. Heidi. Anastasia. Jean. Even Eva. I did miss her and all the fun we had shared. Otherwise, going back to the States seemed pointless. The draft awaited me there and a chance to perish in a Southeast Asian jungle.

I pulled snugly into the sleeping bag and turned my thoughts back to Jean. That would be the life too. Running a vineyard and making love at night to my French lover.

Well, no matter what, the sun would rise tomorrow and life would take care of me. Of that much I had become certain.

I fell asleep late and did not awaken until a truck lumbered down the empty road around midmorning. I sat up, concerned, but no one was there. I lay back down and enjoyed the gentle peace of the countryside. Birds sang. The smell of dew was on the morning air. Far off, I heard the sound of a tractor coming to life. I smiled. I had feared being alone, but now I had passed through those fears. I had no duties or obligations that day, to anyone or anything. I could go wherever I wished.

I finished what was left of the wine for breakfast, brushed my teeth and washed my face alongside the river, placed everything away, rolled up the sleeping bag, relieved myself and started back towards the road. There was a sparkling new gas station beyond the field, with bright new gas pumps. I went inside, bought a loaf of hard crust bread, some jerky and a bottle of water and started down the country road. The elms whispered against the blue sky and white clouds drifted high overhead.

My mind was on Eva's uncle and the lovely summer beaches along the Adriatic. I could picture all the tourists having breakfast right then. That sounded pleasant, being a waiter or a cook with the wind blowing off the sea as I worked.

I cinched the backpack more tightly over my shoulders and started down the road of life, with no idea where it would lead me that day.

Sixteen

A truck driver in his fifties stopped to pick me up just minutes after I had stuck my thumb out. He looked more like a communist party bureaucrat than a truck driver, with a short sleeved plaid shirt and horn rim glasses.

He did not speak much French and even less English so we headed down the road making what conversation we could out of Italian, a few words of French and a lot of hand gestures. We had our windows open and eventually went along without talking at all. The farmland was mostly flat and the day hot and sultry.

When we came to Carmagnola, he pulled off the highway and I was back to hitchhiking. I had stood there for half an hour or so when a young couple stopped to pick me up. They spoke French and were going all the way down to the coast. I asked them everything I could about the place as we went along and they bubbled over with enthusiasm about our destination.

A few miles before the town of Magliano Alpi, the road traversed some hills and from there wound ever higher up into the mountains. I pulled out my map and saw that this was where the arms of the Alps and the Apennines interlocked before melting away into the rocky coastline of Cinque Terra.

An hour later, we came over the crest of a hill and the Ligurian Sea appeared below us, as blue as blue sapphires in the afternoon wind. Lost in the beauty of the coastline, I had completely forgotten myself when the couple came to a stop at the main road. They were turning left up the coast into Savona. Noli was to the west, roughly eight miles the other way.

I thanked them and got out and had been standing there but a few minutes when a young man driving an Aston Martin pulled over. He seemed to be very happy about having an Aston Martin and driving it with the top down and about life in general, and I was very happy that he had stopped to pick me up.

He said something in Italian, which I assumed to be about where I was headed so I mentioned Eva's uncle and asked if he knew of him.

"Oh, si, si," he said.

I gestured to say I was looking for him and he gestured to say, no problem. He would show me the way.

We quickly passed by a small harbor and an area of marine commerce. The road then cleared a point and hugged the coast with the surf lapping at its edge. The rocky cliffs rose up steeply on our right. Ten minutes later, we passed through a tunnel with columns open to the sea on our left side. Then we entered the village of Noli with its ochre and rust colored buildings bounding the waterfront and its ancient castle

211

battlements rising up into the hills. The young man pulled to a stop at the far end of the village and pointed up at a villa clinging to a steep face of the hills. More ancient castle battlements commanded the crest above it.

"Signore Gabriele," he said and pointed at the villa.

"Si?"

"Si. A good man, good man. He help you."

I thanked the young man and climbed out. He drove off with a final wave goodbye.

The cobblestone road leading up the villa was very steep. I went along sweating in the hot sun and wondering if the uncle was there and how he would react to my arrival, if he was.

I came to the towering wooden door of the villa and knocked. A few moments later, an old man answered. I asked if he spoke French. He nodded so I proceeded to tell my tale, as much as seemed necessary. The main point was, I knew the family back in America and was looking for work.

The old man gestured for me to wait and closed the door. Several minutes later, the door was opened again, only this time by a man in his fifties with receding gray hair, blue eyes and a blue sports shirt not tucked into his loosely fitting white cotton pants. He had a phone to his ear and reviewed me with his conversation ongoing in Italian. When the conversation grew heated, the uncle turned away with the phone. There were emphatic gestures and so on. When he looked back, he reviewed me again. Finally, he waved me inside and pointed at a seat in the adjoining room. The décor was casual Mediterranean but smelled of money. The uncle went on arguing with the person on the other end of the phone. With the conversation dragging on and on, he cupped the receiver.

"Have you eaten?" he said in heavily accented English.

I shook my head. He snapped his fingers and the old man reappeared. The uncle rattled off something in rapid fire Italian and the old man gestured for me to follow him. We passed through several rooms and came to a large kitchen. Two women were in there cooking, one of them middle aged, the other one in her twenties. The young one glanced my way several times while the old man gave instructions. The older woman waved for me to have a seat at a massive wooden table. I dropped my pack and sat down.

Before long, I had an antipasto in front of me, along with bread and a glass of wine. This was followed by pasta with sausages. The young woman brought the plates over to me. Our eyes met but we said nothing. When I emptied my wine glass, she filled it again.

"Grazie," I said when I was done.

Both women glanced up from their cooking and went back to it without speaking. I was thinking to ask for the bathroom when the old man appeared and motioned for me to follow him again. We passed back through several rooms and into a study awash in speckled sunlight.

"Please, have a seat," the uncle said from behind his desk.

I did.

"So you know my niece."

I nodded. He smiled wryly. His eyes were very blue, like the color of the sea through the windows.

"You were the one in Paris."

I nodded again. He clicked his tongue.

"Too bad. I have tried my best with my brother over the years, but there is no changing him. He is an inveterate bourgeois American now."

I explained my earlier idea of coming to seek his help with Eva. He nodded.

"And I would have helped you, but you are dreaming. Eva, she is nothing if not shrewd. You are not about to separate her from the family fortune."

"I know that now."

"Good. Best not to have any illusions."

I nodded.

"So, I understand you are looking for work."

"Yes."

"And what can you do?"

"I've worked in restaurants, mostly. As a cook. I've waited on tables a bit too."

He scratched at his chin like the godfather and made a very slight gesture with his hand.

"I know someone in town with a restaurant."

He took out a piece of paper and jotted down a note.

"The name of the restaurant is Pompanos. The man is called Ernesto. Give him this and he will take care of you."

I took the piece of paper, looked at the writing in Italian and thanked him.

"And a place to stay?" he said with a gesture at my pack. "You are camping?"

"I have been."

He nodded.

"There is a guest house out back you can use for now. How long were you thinking to stay?"

"I don't know. I don't have a ticket back to the States."

"Ahhhhhhh," he said. "I see. I understand now. You really are in love with my niece."

I nodded.

"Well, maybe not so much now," he added with another wry smile. "And are you willing to start right away?"

I nodded.

"Good. I'll have Umberto show you to the guest house." He gestured as if to show me how to shave and clean up. "Maybe a bit, eh? Before you go to meet with Ernesto."

"Thank you. I will."

He snapped his fingers and the old man reappeared. The uncle stood up and held out his hand.

"Augusto."

"Paul."

"Paulo. If you are hungry, just go see them in the kitchen. If you need anything else, come see me."

"Thanks."

He gestured with both hands.

"There are worse places in this world to be stranded."

He spoke to Umberto, gestured for me to follow and went back to the business on his desk.

Umberto led me out past a pool in back and through a garden and up the hill along some winding stone steps. The guest house was tucked away among the trees but had a fine view of the sea. Umberto opened the door and gestured for me to make myself at home.

"Signore Gabriele, he tells me to take you to meet the owner of Pompanos."

"Okay. Can you give me fifteen minutes?"

"I will be waiting out front."

"Thank you."

He went out and closed the door. I flopped down on the bed feeling goddamned luxurious all of a sudden. I got up on my elbows and looked out the windows. The sea was like a jewel out there in the distance. I fell back on the bed and pumped both fists.

Yes! You made it, you dumb son of a bitch!

Having shaved and showered, I dug out the cleanest clothing I could unearth and splashed on a bit of cologne from the bathroom. As offered, Umberto was waiting for me out in front of the villa and we drove into town with the sea off to our right now and the rugged hills rising up steeply to our left and everything lovely under the sun.

At the restaurant, I handed the note to a woman at the desk in front. She looked at the note and guided me to a table on the veranda outside. I had grown lost in the beauty of the sea when Ernesto appeared. He was medium height, stout and reminded me of an old fisherman, but one that smelled of cologne.

"Signore Gabriele says you can cook."

"Yes."

"And wait on tables?"

"I've not done it much but I can."

He said something in Italian. I stared.

"You don't speak Italian."

I shook my head.

"French. And English."

"Okay. For now, I'll have you bus tables. You can help with any Americans who only speak English. If I need you in the kitchen, I'll call. Are you ready to start right away?"

I nodded

"All right. Come. I'll get you a shirt and you can start by cleaning up this table."

Tossed into the fire, I was quickly treated like a baby brother by all the women but like an intruder by most of the men. When I jumped in to help with the dishes, one of the cooks tossed his pots into the sink, splashing me with dirty water. Mariella, one of the waitresses, got into a heated argument with him over it. Ernesto came in and gave everyone hell for arguing. When people argued in Italian, it really got your attention.

Mariella brought me a fresh shirt and patted me sweetly on the cheek.

"Lui è solo un bambino."

The other women smiled. The cook who had it out for me made a big racket with the pans in response.

I went back out to check the tables and Julietta, another one of the waitresses, had me help her out with an American couple. Anything extra that came up, I did it without asking and the evening flew by. At one point, I caught Ernesto glancing my way with an approving look.

At two in the morning, the women had me join them for a glass of wine on the dining terrace in back. The sea was black and bristling white below us. A few of the men had joined the women and talked among themselves. I listened to all the conversations, straining to understand Italian.

At one point, Mariella looked my way.

"Why you here?"

I shook my head, thinking how difficult it would be for me to answer that question in English, let alone French.

"Amor," I thought to say.

"Amore?"

That got the lady's attention.

"Quale? What girl? Where is dis girl?"

I motioned to say, gone. All the women said "Awwwwwww," in unison.

The men kept stealing glances my way. The women were busy talking among themselves but I could tell it was about me. The general tone seemed to be, poor little Paulo. All alone in the world. I sipped my wine and tried to look very alone in the world.

"Where you stay?" Mariella said.

"With Signore Gabriele."

Her eyes got big. Everyone's did.

"Signore Gabriele?" Mariella said. "No. How you know Signore Gabriele?"

"Amore," I said.

"No! Sua figlia? His daughter?"

"No, no. His niece."

"Ohhhhhhh."

The women resumed their animated discussion with frequent looks my way.

"The niece, she Americano?" Julietta said.

I nodded.

"So why she leave you?"

I shook my head. What the hell was I going to tell them? Beyond Eva's inheritance, I had no idea what had gone down in Paris. Some kind of subterfuge I did not pretend to understand.

I made a gesture, as if smoking a pipe.

"Do you like?" I asked of everyone in French.

"Hascisc?" Mariella said. She looked at the men and back at me. "You want to buy?"

"No, no." I patted my pocket. "I have some."

The men looked impressed.

"You?" Mariella asked again.

I nodded.

"We just need a pipe."

When I went to retrieve the hash from my pocket, she waved emphatically. There was a quick discussion with the men and one of them went back into the now darkened restaurant. He returned shortly and waved as if to say, the coast was clear.

"It's okay now," Mariella said to me.

While I pulled out the hash, one of the men produced a pipe. I packed the bowl full and he lit it for me. The pipe went around the terrace with everyone taking hits and coughing. Within a few minutes, the whole crew was high and laughing.

I stared out to sea, content. I had a job. I had a place to live. I had a pack of lovely young women worrying over me. I looked back and saw Mariella staring.

"È soltanto un ragazzino," she said.

The other women were smiling. The men laughed.

"What?" I said.

Mariella rustled my hair. One of the men said something to her. She looked back at me.

"He want to know, where you get this?"

I shrugged and explained about Mickey and my life on Formentera. The latter got them buzzing. From the sounds of it, half of the men were ready to relocate. All they could see was cheap hashish. They didn't seem to care about La Guarda taking over the island.

Later, the ladies gave me a ride home in Julietta's car and remained parked in the driveway, waiting to see if I actually went inside. I waved a final time and heard them drive off as I disappeared through the servant's entrance at the side of the villa.

All was dark and quiet around in back. I followed the stone steps up to the guest house, slipped inside and flopped onto the bed, exhausted. I fell asleep wrapped up in the bedspread with my clothes still on.

At noon the next day, I was back for another hectic shift at Pompanos. Things never lacked for excitement. The hours flew by with me running back and forth. I quickly learned a bit of Italian and gathered together with the others again late that night out on the terrace, smoking hashish, drinking wine and talking of life.

On my first day off, two weeks later, I went down to the kitchen around midmorning and found the older woman not there, only the younger one. She looked up from her cooking and then at the clock.

"Vuoi colazione o pranzo?" she said.

I shrugged.

"Non capisco," I said.

I had learned how to say that much early on at the restaurant.

"Brekafest," she said.

"Hmm, yeah. Breakfast," I said.

While the caffè latte was brewing, she put out a plate of rolls, with butter, and jam, and also several pieces of fette biscottate. I tried the biscottate and quickly gulped down the caffè latte when it arrived.

Her service to me concluded, the young woman went back to her cooking. I stared at her, reminded of the peasant cook in Fellini's *La Strada*. Dark, lean and brooding; not beautiful but not hard to look at. When I was full and done with the caffè latte, I took the cup and passed close to the young woman's backside on my way to the sink. She did not look up but her hands stopped for that brief moment. I set the cup down and stepped up close behind her.

"Come see me," I whispered in her ear.

She looked over her shoulder with the fierceness of a jaguar. I smiled ever so slightly and touched my nose to her ear.

Before I went out of the kitchen, I looked back. She looked at me and quickly went back to her cooking.

Up at the guest house, I left the door part way open and lay on the bed, dreaming. Some minutes later, she appeared at the door and let herself in with a look back down at the main villa. I got up and stared. Her dark eyes stared back as if searching my soul. When I kissed her lips, there was a brief pause before her passions erupted in full flame. She was soon on top of me, riding like a gazelle across the wild savannah. She made little noise, only what a steed would make while galloping. I saw her ears flush suddenly and felt the sweat bead on the small of her back and knew she was coming. I came a few seconds later and we collapsed together in the warm, dry air.

Later, while kissing her goodbye at the door, she slapped me gently on the cheek and stared with those dark eyes. When she was gone, I lay back on the bed and dreamed of wild gazelles.

Late that afternoon, I was off to drink in the town when Signore Gabriele came out from his office door and waved for me to join him. I did.

"Sit, sit," he said.

We stared at each other from across his desk.

"There is a saying in Italy. You don't shit where you eat. I'm sure it's the same everywhere."

I felt my ears burn, knowing he had seen us. He gestured as if to say, it was no big deal, but not particularly welcome around the villa.

I nodded. Signore Gabriele picked up an envelope from his desk, bit his lower lip and stared as if preparing to tell a soldier's wife she was now a widow. He tapped the envelope several times on the desk before handing it over to me.

I saw immediately that it was from Eva.

"I'm sorry. I made the mistake of mentioning this to her mother and…"

He shrugged. My impulse was to hurry off and read it but Signore Gabriele clearly had something else on his mind, so I waited.

"When I was your age, there was a young woman. My god, the obsession. I think I would have chased her into the sun. At the same time, I was presented with an opportunity to sail around the world on a grand expedition. It was the chance of a lifetime, but no, I had to chase after this woman instead."

Signore Gabriele scratched his receding hairline with just the baby and ring fingers of his right hand. He shrugged fatalistically before going on.

"Of course, there are always more opportunities in life, but after all these years, it is the one thing I find myself regretting."

I stared.

"I know, I know," he said. "Nothing I say will dissuade you. I can see it in your eyes. The same obsession has bitten you. But I would encourage you to think long and hard before making any decisions. Look around you. You have already made a wonderful life for yourself here. I spoke with Ernesto and he is very, very happy with your work. What are you going to do? Run back and start a family and become like Eva's parents?"

We stared.

"Trust me. I am very fond of my niece but...well...this is for you to decide. You know you are welcome here, for as long as you like."

"Thank you."

He nodded.

"Go. Go read your letter...And..." He waved in the general direction of the kitchen. "Be...you know..."

I nodded and got up to leave.

Seventeen

A ware now that Signore Gabriele had been keeping an eye on me, I walked back up the stone steps to the guest house as if I couldn't care less about Eva's letter. But the minute I had closed the door behind myself, I rushed to the bed and ripped open the envelope.

'Dearest Paul...', Eva had started her note and went on to share a bit about what had happened after we parted in Paris, then how things were going in college but quickly moved on to how much she loved and missed me and how touched she was by my courage. She was especially happy to learn that I had found her uncle and thought it would be really groovy if she could come visit with me during her Christmas break. That was now less than three months away. Of course, if I decided to come home before then, she asked me to stop in North Carolina. She wanted to see me. She really missed me and was sorry if she had hurt me in any way and would make it all up the next time we met.

I stared out at the sea, a spell cast over me, just like Signore Gabriele had said. What kind of spell was another question.

The next day at work, the women immediately noticed the change in me.

"Si è sotto un incantesimo," Mariella said passing by me. She gestured with one finger. "What's a wrong, Paulo? A spell?"

When we gathered after work that night, she took my hand and looked at the chewed fingernails, then into my eyes.

"You...the spell," she said.

I pulled my hand away and went back to calculating things. How much money would I need to get back to New York? I probably had enough to buy a ticket, but then I would be broke. From Eva's own words, I knew there was an alternative. If I went to the consulate in Milan and pleaded hardship, they would repatriate me.

Over the next few days, I did my best to reason through things and heed Signore Gabriele's words of advice, but to no avail. The fever was in me. When the concerned looks and frequent questions from the women wore on me too much, I barked at them.

At the end of the week, Signore Gabriele flew off to Palermo on business. I used the opportunity to take my last paycheck and steal away without saying goodbye — to him or anyone. I sensed the dangerous nature of my impulses but could not seem to kick them and did not want to be burdened with any questions.

That day, on my way over the mountains, while waiting alongside the road for a ride, the sky grew dark and an autumn squall suddenly stirred up. Thunder tore at the heavens. The elm trees howled wildly in the wind. I raced for the cover of a pine tree by the side of the road and huddled there, growing wet and miserable.

Thinking it must be an omen, I considered turning back. I wanted to shout at the sky. What is wrong with me!? Why am I so obsessed with this woman!?

Everything seemed so far away and beyond my reach.

Feeling defeated by my own emotions, I broke down and wept, my tears washed by the rain.

When the sky finally cleared that afternoon, I dug out some dry clothes and went back further among the trees to change. I was unsure of anything anymore but the inertia of my decision kept drawing me forward.

It was well after dark that evening when I got into Milan. Given the hour, I made do with a cheap meal in a corner restaurant and slept in a park. In the morning I located the embassy. A receptionist listened to my story and told me to have a seat.

Some minutes later, a sympathetic but formal woman in her thirties invited me into her office. There was a process within the State Department, I was told. If my application for repatriation was approved, a voucher for a plane flight home would follow. Sometimes the process took a few days, sometimes a week. In the interim, the consulate would pay for my lodgings. It was my obligation to return every day to check on my status.

On the way out, the woman provided me with a voucher for the room and a list of nearby places. The consulate would pay anything up to roughly thirty American dollars per night. She also handed me several brochures. There were many wonderful museums and cathedrals and sights to see in Milan. I should use the opportunity to enjoy them.

I went back out to the streets, intent on finding a room first. I wanted to shower and sleep in a bed. Checking the addresses against my map, I headed for the nearest one and found it on a backstreet. The owner ran a small shoe repair shop on the ground level. The stairwell to the flat was between his storefront and a diner next door. The owner said something to his wife in the shoe shop and led me upstairs. The stairwell was dimly lit. The walls were lined with paisley wallpaper that had turned the color of umber over the years.

On the second floor, we went down a short hallway with four doors. The owner opened the last one on the right. The floors were wooden, the old varnish darkened by the years. There was a bed by the window and an old dresser by the closet door. A sink hung from one corner of the wall. If you wanted to use the toilet, it was down the hall. Otherwise, the room was clean. A bum would have loved it. I nodded and gave the owner the voucher. He said something about being quiet and left. I immediately went down the hall to take a shower and thereafter collapsed on the bed.

I was awakened late that afternoon by the sounds of the city and a sudden sense of déjà vu. It seemed as if I had been in this same exact room countless times over the ages, waiting for a way to get back home.

I got up and looked out the window. The backside of brick apartment buildings faced me from across a large courtyard. A couple of kids were down in the courtyard playing. Makeshift catwalks connected most of the opposing rooftops. Clotheslines hung from the balconies, draped with drying clothes. Caruso was crooning away somewhere. I heard a couple arguing.

I went back to lie on the bed and pictured the scene; a loutish husband seated at the kitchen table, black hair spilling out his tank top, his wife sweating over a hot stove. Most of the time, she was giving it to him. Now and then, he yelled back at her. Sometimes they were both yelling. Whatever it was, they weren't happy. That or they loved arguing.

I lay there taking in every sight and sound, swept away by the mystery of life in a foreign land.

Then the impending repatriation returned to my thoughts. The whole thing felt like a surrender. A few days ago, I was waiting tables in Noli, as happy as hell and feeling pretty immortal. Now those feelings were nowhere to be found.

Love did strange things to people. Women rent their clothes. Sane men took their own lives. Empires ground to a halt.

I knew this and that my impulses were not really healthy for me but felt powerless to stop them. I could not seem to get the hunger out of my heart. I saw Eva's beauty, remembered our tender and irreplaceable moments together and was prepared to cross a thousand galaxies to get back to her.

Tired of my own thoughts, I freshened up at the sink in my room and headed downstairs to the little diner. Inside, I found four people busy at their meals, two old men at one table and a middle-aged couple at another. They offered polite nods my way as I came in and went back to their own business. I sat by a window and stared out. Dusk had settled over the streets.

The owner's wife came out from the kitchen. She spoke French and took my order. Out of kindness, she added a sausage to my plate of pasta and brought me a basket of bread. When I had consumed the first basket, she brought me another. I washed all that down with two glasses of red wine and went outside to smoke a Gauloises.

After some thought, I started off towards Parco Sempione. I had heard this was where the young people gathered at night.

The city seemed empty with summer over and most of the tourists gone home. Nostalgia for America joined Eva in plaguing me; roadside hamburger joints, a day at the beach with suntan lotion and transistor radios. I would have given a lot just to hear someone speak English.

After walking a mile or so, I came to Piazza Duomo. It swarmed with people, out enjoying the evening. The front steps of all the adjacent apartment buildings were overflowing with families. Voices, laughter and music filled the air.

I crossed over to where a metro station bordered the plaza. People were coming and going from Parco Sempione across the street. I leaned against a lamp post and watched.

Out of the crowd, I heard a man speaking English with a Bronx accent and moved in that direction. Hearing the voice again, I made out the man and stopped several feet away. He was black-haired and swarthy and seemed to be arguing a matter of great importance with three other men, sometimes in English, sometimes in Italian. Eventually one of them noticed me staring so I walked over and introduced myself.

"Paul," I said. "Sorry to butt in but I've been dying just to talk to someone in English."

"Fuhgeddaboudit," the swarthy man said with a firm handshake and a grip on my shoulder.

"Did you hear that, youse clowns? Another Yank, so you can fuhgeddaboudit giving me any more shit. All right?"

"The name's Tony," he said to me. "This is Ian, Arrigo and Janek. Foreign degenerates, one and all."

We shook hands all around.

By their names and voices alone, I quickly knew something about them. Ian was British and had the long, curly locks and frail physique of a Limey rocker. Arrigo was from Sicily, though with his goatee and pork-pie hat, he looked more like a New Yorker than Tony and Janek was Czechoslovakian. As with Irenka and Nikola, he was a refugee from the Soviet invasion. You saw them all over Europe, blown away by the wind, the look of shock still on their faces.

"Ian here just got back from England," Tony was explaining to me. "So we're trying to decide. Have some dinner or get some hashish first."

At this, I explained about Formentera.

"Fuhgeddaboudit," Tony said. "Everyone's walking around with an ounce of hash? So where's your stash?"

"Smoked it all back in Noli."

"You hear that?" Tony said to Arrigo

Tony said something to Arrigo in Italian and gave him a playful shove.

"Arrigo here's my cousin," Tony said. "We's family from way back. Right, Henry?"

Arrigo said a few sharp words back, which only broadened Tony's smile.

"Let's have a bit of the oobly boobly then," Ian said. "I'm in a bit of a funk after the long train ride."

"Then oobly boobly it is," Tony said and off he went down the sidewalk, playfully bantering with the taciturn Arrigo. Ian, Janek and I fell in behind them.

Given Janek's lousy English and lack of French, I struck up a conversation with Ian and learned that he was an artist with a gig doing airbrush work for a photography studio. I had no idea why photos would need to be airbrushed but Ian assured me that some did.

Up ahead, Tony and Arrigo had dashed across the busy boulevard prompting Ian, Janek and me to follow suit. Tony was already seated behind the wheel of a parked Fiat when we ran up, with Arrigo riding shotgun. The three of us crowded into the backseat. Tony wasted no time in starting the Fiat and racing away from the curb. When he failed to check for passing traffic, I instinctively sat forward.

A few blocks up ahead, Tony cut onto a narrow winding lane, not much wider than the car, and increased his speed to fifty miles an hour. I sat farther forward in the seat. Tony looked back at me with a big smile. If another car had suddenly appeared going the other way, we would all be dead. Arrigo seemed indifferent to the danger. Ian shrugged when I looked his way. Janek alone seemed to share my fears.

I was grateful to see the narrow lane return to a main boulevard. Tony turned right and right again a few blocks later onto a quiet, residential street and parked. Arrigo got out, climbed the steps to a three-story building and disappeared inside.

While we waited, Ian spoke quietly with Janek in German. Tony listened to them for a moment then spoke to me about how his family in New York was involved with Arrigo's family in Sicily.

"It's a big olive oil business," Tony said with a wink.

When Arrigo returned, Tony started the Fiat and sped over to Ian's flat in the same mad fashion. I had one hand clamped on the armrest.

Ian's upstairs loft was basically one large room that looked the way you would expect an artist's place to look—an easel with oil paintings and charcoal sketches pinned all over the walls. A large drafting table sat against one wall with photographs suspended from clips all around it. The top of the drafting table was littered with Ian's airbrush tools.

He rummaged around in the chaos at the base of his drafting table and found a water pipe. Arrigo pulled out the hash. Tony packed the bowl full and everyone took turns getting high. Amidst the ensuing laughter and irreverent conversation, I was asked to explain how I had ended up in Europe. Love and war were involved, the woman I was determined to see again and the war I was trying to avoid.

"It is same in my country too," Janek observed. "Everyone leave because of war, and leave love behind. Many, many unhappy people."

Tony, who had been lying on the couch, fell to his knees and pleaded in a mock Italian accent.

" Please don't a go. I love a you so much."

"Tony wouldn't know about these things," Ian commented dryly. "He's only in love with himself."

"That's right," Tony said and returned to his prone position on the couch. "Hey, I just had this vision!" He gestured up at the ceiling as if painting on it. "See, there are these two armies approaching each other on a battlefield. You know, like ancient Rome or something. Shields up. Swords at the ready. It's getting on towards the end of day and the two armies are so close they can almost touch each other. Then, at the last minute, one of the soldiers calls out, 'Hey! What do you say we screw this bullshit and go get laid in town'?"

Ian and I chuckled over Tony's absurd story.

"No, seriously. See, they just throw down their swords and march off and the generals are standing there going, 'Hey! Hey! Wait a minute! We got a war going on here'!"

I chuckled again. Janek stared, not understanding until Ian explained the joke and he smirked. Only Arrigo sat there humorless. When I looked at him, he stared coldly back at me. Tony tried making various funny faces but nothing worked on Arrigo.

"Eh, screw this bullshit. Let's go get laid," Tony said to more laughter.

Eventually, the conversation turned to politics and the state of the world and inevitably to talk of hunger. Tony suggested we dash out for a bite to eat. The prospect of another wild toad ride aside, I was onboard. Even Ian, who had entered an opium like trance from the hashish, rose to his feet.

Tony got behind the wheel and the previous madness resumed. I was giddy by the time we arrived at a restaurant that Ian had recommended. With the late hour, it was already closing, and seeing us barge in through the front door, the disconcerted owner told us as much. We were offered a table and a liter of red wine as consolation. As to the kitchen, it was closed. Ian spoke with Tony about finding another restaurant.

Arrigo was staring at the owner, not the least bit content with the answer he had received.

The owner returned a few moments later, did the courtesy of pouring everyone a glass of wine and started off again. Arrigo called out to him in Italian and the owner reluctantly returned, wiping at his apron. Arrigo let on by way of a few gentle words and gestures, that we did not expect anything fancy, maybe just some pasta and bread with our wine. Arrigo pointed to a couple against the far wall. Why not? They were still eating. The waiters were still there.

The owner acknowledged this with a respectful nod, but the answer was still no. The kitchen was closed. While the waiters put out their fresh linens and tableware, we were welcome to finish our wine. Then? The owner gestured at the door as if to say, it would be time to go.

Turning to leave, he had gotten perhaps three paces when Arrigo barked out something in Italian and everything in the restaurant ground to a halt, the waiters, the couple eating in the corner, even those of us at the table. Meanwhile, the owner had turned back to face Arrigo as one does a firing squad. Arrigo allowed time to stand still for a few moments before making a brusque gesture with his right hand, his right palm facing out from his body and turning swiftly back inwards and the suddenly obsequious owner shuffled back over to our table.

The waiters, not wanting to make the owner's business their business, resumed their work and the couple went back to eating, albeit a bit more quietly now.

With the owner leaning over the table, Arrigo whispered in his ear. The owner nodded to everything that was said and scurried off towards the kitchen, snapping fingers at the waiters and letting it be known by way of gestures that our wish was their command.

I looked at Arrigo, having a pretty good idea what was behind the hand gesture. He was Mafia and there were two things you did not do when it came to the Cosa Nostra. Cross them, or ask about their personal affairs. Each time Arrigo's stare turned my way, I half expected him to make the gesture at me.

A few minutes later, an antipasto was delivered to our table, followed by a pasta dish with red sauce and meatballs, then a veal plate, along with all the wine and bread we could eat.

Very late that night, Tony dropped me back at my room. Arrigo stared forward without saying a word but all the other boys wished me well. Tony told me they were heading to Genoa in a few days and maybe on to the French Alps. I was welcome to join them. I thanked him for the invitation but declined and watched them drive away.

Late the next afternoon, I stopped by the consulate and learned that my flight home to New York had been arranged in two days. Despite my growing ambivalence, the inertia of my decision kept propelling me forward.

On my way back down to the street, I was joined by a thirtyish Italian interpreter leaving work for the day. He was slim and urbane with thinning hair combed straight back.

"Alfredo," he said and offered me his hand.

"Paul," I said.

"Eh, Paulo. Come va?"

"Bene, bene."

As it was in any language, you pretended to be doing great, even if you were down on your luck.

We had come to the lobby entrance and Alfredo opened the door for me. We went out onto the dusky streets. Alfredo asked me my reasons for being at the consulate and I told him. I was all alone in his country and nearly broke and had asked to be repatriated.

"Eh, you are coming home for dinner with me then," Alfredo said dramatically. "My wife, she always makes enough for an army."

He had said this last with a gesture to suggest mountains of food.

Relieved at the prospect of company and a good meal, I readily agreed.

Alfredo led me off the main boulevard and into a district of grand old apartment buildings shaded by trees. Arriving at a particular one, Alfredo opened the vestibule door for me. At his front door on the third floor, he winked and knocked. A few moments later, his beautiful wife opened it, wearing a white blouse, black skirt and black high heels. She was petite, sweet and effervescent in equal measures, with pale skin set against black hair.

"Paulo, my wife Regina," he said, introducing us. "Regina, Paulo."

While Regina shook my hand, Alfredo rattled off a string of sentences in rapid fire Italian. Regina turned to me with a warm sympathetic smile.

"Come, come," she said and showed me the way to the bathroom. "You clean up and we eat."

When I returned, Regina made me comfortable at the dinner table. Alfredo had placed some romantic string music on the stereo, the atmosphere suddenly that of early sixties era Sinatra. The romance of young couples was in the air.

Regina went off to the kitchen and returned with a plate of marinated albacore, an antipasto and a bowl of fresh grapes. She encouraged me to eat and ran back to the kitchen. Alfredo and I were lost in conversation when Regina returned with the pasta course. I was already full.

With Alfredo acting as interpreter, Regina asked me to explain how I had arrived in Europe. When she heard the love story, she swooned.

"Ohhhh," she said. "Amor."

Love was the same everywhere, in all languages.

Soon, Regina was off to retrieve the main course of veal cutlets. We talked until late over aperitifs and coffee. I still felt gorged when I arrived home to my backstreet flat. It was a cool autumn night in Milan and I lay there in the darkness of my room, thinking of Regina. If only I could find a gal like that, someone who would swoon over my chivalrous intentions. I saw her black eyes and beautiful, caring face in my mind's eye and wanted a woman to be there for me, the way she was there for her husband — dinner at dusk, Mantovani playing in the background and the feeling of eternity in our hearts.

Through my open window, I heard the same couple arguing across the way. That was what I did not want, where love was a futile battle of wills, a lifetime wasted on a war that could never be won.

I thought of Eva then. Would we be happy for a lifetime, like Alfredo and Regina? The memory of Paris haunted me, the secret that Tanya and all of them had failed to speak. I recoiled from what was perhaps best left unsaid. I grew depressed again at the idea of rushing home. To what? Something told me this headlong journey was a fool's errand. Why not just head off to Genoa and the Alps with Tony and his gang? Or go find Jean? Or just go back to my happy life at Signore Gabriele's place

I tossed and turned all night and finally fell asleep very late, no closer to being at peace in my heart.

Eighteen

I awakened in the morning still at war with my emotions. The fever for Eva was now overlaid with a general homesickness, my heart drawn back by the memories of old friends and familiar places. There was little in the way of logic to it.

I eventually shaved and showered and dressed. I had one last look around the room before heading out the door. Caruso was crooning off in the distance, the same couple arguing. They never seemed to stop, their rancor immersed in a general cacophony of blaring TVs and dozens of conversations in Italian. You could never find peace in that place, but I would never forget it.

At the consulate, I was asked to fill out several forms before finally receiving my airline voucher. A shuttle was waiting for me out in front. The staff wished me well before I headed down to the street.

At the airport, amidst the bustle of fellow travelers, I felt a powerful urge to turn back. Why not continue on with my grand adventure? Mine was now the march of the defeated.

Pulled forward by inertia and little else, I boarded the DC-10, found my seat and waited for the flight to take off. Once in the air, I ordered a drink and then another. With the six hour time difference and a roughly nine hour nonstop flight, we would be landing in New York around two in the afternoon. I planned to call Eva in North Carolina first thing. Beyond that, I had no idea what I was doing.

Arriving to customs in New York, I was suddenly gripped with terror. I looked like a poster boy for the Haight-Ashbury district and had two grams of hashish from Tony tucked away in my shoe.

I remembered somebody telling me once, just smile and act like you don't have a care in the world. I did and the customs agent waved me right through.

Down in the terminal, I found a phone booth and dialed Eva's number. After many rings, a young woman answered. I explained the reason for my call and was told to wait. She would go check. The phone was the dorm phone and Eva was down the hall.

A minute later, Eva came on the phone.

"Paul. Where are you?"

"New York."

She sort of screamed.

"So, what am I doing?" I said.

"Go home and I'll see you there."

"What do you mean go home? And wait there until Christmas?"

"No, no. My father's been in the hospital and my older sister's getting married so I received a two week bereavement leave. I'm flying back in three days."

"Okay."

There was a pause.

"I love you," she said.

"I love you too."

"I can't wait to hear all about your adventure."

"Yeah. Fun at Signore Gabriele's."

She laughed. The operator rang through, saying I would need to deposit another dollar seventy-five in twenty seconds.

"Okay," Eva said when the operator was gone. "Just call me at my folk's place in three days."

"I'm sure. If I learned anything from this trip, it's that they don't want me around."

"Just call. I already told my Mom that I planned to see you and she won't interfere. She just told me not to say anything to my father."

"All right. I'll see you in three days."

"I can't wait," she said.

"Yeah, me too."

I was about to say something else but the phone went dead. I placed the black receiver back in place and stood there staring off into the distance.

Exhausted from the long journey and wanting to sleep, I considered getting a room for the night but decided to look into flights first and walked over to the United desk. The attendant checked her schedule and said she had one going out to LA in roughly an hour and it was only half booked. The price was $85. I paid her and made my way up to the airport bar to wait.

It was getting on towards sunset when we landed in LA. I caught a bus down south to the old town. I had two hundred dollars left in my pocket and rented a room. It was a toss-up between sleeping or taking a shower first and sleep won out.

I awakened a few hours later in the shadows of dusk, feeling lost and depressed about being back home. The suburban sprawl of my youth had always felt a bit heartless and still did. I had just traded a magical journey across the Seven Seas for miles and miles of asphalt and commercial clutter.

I showered and went out to the streets, looking for some of my old friends. After several calls from a phone booth, I located a guy named Chris and he drove over to pick me up.

"Wow, far out, man," he said as I climbed into his car. "Tell me all about your trip."

I gave him an overview, without the women involved. It was a small town and whatever I said was bound to get back to Eva.

"Wow, brother. Why did you even come back?"

I shrugged. Besides Eva, I had no idea.

We stopped to have a burger and then drove up into the hills behind town. The last light of day glowed along the western horizon and the stars had started to come out.

Several of my old friends were gathered out in the middle of Dump Road. It was called that because it had once led to the town dump. They had since moved the dump and it was now just a road going nowhere. We were surrounded by orange groves and rows of towering eucalyptus trees. The humps of the nearby hills were visible above the trees, now black in the growing twilight.

I got out and exchanged greetings with everyone.

"Far out. Europe. Wow. Tell us all about it."

While we smoked some of my hashish, I told them about the trip and especially about living on Formentera.

"Wow! We should go there and start an import business," this one guy said.

"I already told you. It's too late. Anyway, if you want cheap hashish, just go to Marrakesh. That's where they make it."

As the conversation rambled on, I stood back from the scene. It was like we were doing the same thing we had been doing in high school, only we weren't in high school anymore.

Late that night, we ended up out by the river, gathered in a circle and doing a tribal dance in the moonlight. From where we stood, I could see across the valley and up to the knoll and my old campsite.

I hung around waiting for Eva to show up two days later. Some friends and I were in the living room of an old house near my rented room, listening to the first Jethro Tull album when she came in. Eva said hello to everyone before we went outside together and kissed in the warm, Indian summer like night. Eva was wearing jeans with high heel sandals. Her hair was up on her head. We searched each other's eyes in the darkness. She seemed more mature now.

"So, tell me all about the rest of your trip."

"Let's go to my room."

"Okay."

The old lady who ran the place was a bit fussy so I had Eva take off her heels before we tiptoed up the wooden stairs. Safely back in my room, we wasted no time in tearing off our clothes. Later, we were lying naked in the warm evening air, touching each other and staring up at the ceiling.

"It reminds me of Paris," Eva said.

"Yeah."

And Paris reminded me of Tanya's secret.

Eva shook me.

"So, tell me all about your trip."

I did, again leaving out the women. Eva got up on one elbow all of a sudden and asked rhetorically.

"And you never met one woman?"

I smirked.

"That's a silly question. Of course I met women but nothing happened."

"Sure."

I shrugged.

"It sounds like it was a lot of fun."

I shrugged again.

"Sometimes. Sometimes I was very lonely."

"Were you ever scared?" she said with a look into my eyes.

"Sometimes. It would have been a lot different if you had come with me."

"We could do something like that after college."

"You don't need college to go live in Europe. I already told you. Your uncle will help us. Hell, we could go to college over there."

"Maybe," she said with a kiss and curled back up in my arms. "Are you coming to North Carolina?"

"To do what?"

"To be with me."

"And do what?"

"You could go to junior college and start on a degree. They have a really good educational system."

"Okay," I said.

I was game. I had no idea why I loved that woman the way I did, but I did. Enough to move to North Carolina. Eva was silent but I could feel her mind working in the moonlight.

Later, she kissed me and got up to dress.

Over the next few days, Eva was busy with her family but we saw each other every night. Several times, I was about to ask about the unspoken secret but always stopped short of doing so.

That week, my sister Angela tracked me down by phone at a friend's house and invited me to a birthday party she was throwing for her husband Rick. With the whole family expected to be there, including my parents, I was reluctant to go. I hadn't seen them since the old man had kicked me out of the house.

"Just let it go," Angela said.

"Yeah, easy for you to say."

"Look, I want you to be there. You've never seen your new nephew Blake and your niece Cynthia hardly knows you. She's going to be three in a couple of weeks."

"Look, I just don't want to get in a fight with the old man."

Angela sighed.

"Just come, okay? If he gets out of hand, I'll kick him in the shin."

"All right. I'll talk to Eva about it."

"But you'll come."

"Yeah, I guess."

"Okay, I'm holding you to it. I'm dying to hear all about your trip."

I got off the phone thinking I wouldn't go but when Eva learned about the party, she insisted we attend. She knew my sister from our school days but had never met my parents. I had preferred it that way, especially when it came to the old man.

It turned out that my sister and my brother in law were renting a Craftsman home in the old part of town, just a few blocks from my room. Eva and I arrived that Saturday night with a present for Rick. Angela greeted us at the door and was quickly chatting away with Eva. My mother welcomed us in and gave me a big hug.

"My baby," she said with tears in her eyes. "And this is your girlfriend?"

"Yeah. Eva, this is my Mom, Gina. Mom, this is Eva."

My mother made a sign, like va va voom. Eva laughed. Over Eva's shoulder, I saw the old man. He always had a drink in his hand, and was always full of diplomatic charm when working a crowd.

In a further act of diplomacy, Angela dragged Eva over to meet him. Out came the Irish charm. For beautiful women, he was the nicest guy in the world.

"So, the big world traveler," he said to me when I got near.

"Don't start," my mother said on her way out to the kitchen.

Angela brought over her new baby Blake for me to see.

"Isn't he adorable?"

"Yeah," I said.

He was all pink and wrinkled and asleep. I looked down at my niece Cynthia, who was hiding behind Angela's dress.

"And you remember your Uncle Paul?" she said.

Cynthia hid further behind my sister. I went to retrieve a drink from the kitchen. Rick was out there, making one of his own.

"Hey," he said.

Rick was a laid-back kind of guy. Never an emotion.

"Whatever you want." He sipped from his drink. "I hear you had a cool time."

"Yeah, it was a trip."

"You should be going to college," my mother said from the stove.

She hadn't bothered looking over her shoulder. I tipped my drink at Rick and headed for the living room. My brother Patrick was just arriving with his girlfriend and said hello. Other people were piling in through the door. Amidst the growing madhouse, I ended up in a corner telling Rick about my journey. Eva came over and sat on the arm of my chair and we had a few laughs about our wild nights in Paris. I was telling Rick about my stay with Eva's uncle when my mother called out that the dinner was ready.

While we ate, I fielded more questions about the trip but for the most part the talk had turned to family and friends and the changing times. A new President, the Black Panthers, cities being burned to the ground. One of Angela's friends had been to Woodstock and there was talk about that. The sixties were about to turn to the seventies and the war was still on everyone's mind.

Miraculously, I escaped that night without getting into it with the old man. Eva and I drove down the beach and hung out at a club until late, listening to music. We stopped at my place and made love before she drove home.

When it came time for her sister's wedding, we decided it would be best if I stayed away. A few days later, there was a complication with her father's health. I didn't see Eva that night or the following one and then it was time for her to go back to North Carolina.

We met on a Friday night. She was flying out the next day so she would have Sunday to get ready for school again. I felt empty about her departure. The dark secret from her past still hung over our every word. We made love in my room but it wasn't enough. I still wanted answers.

"Are you coming?" Eva said before kissing me goodbye.

"I guess."

She shook me.

"What?"

"What? I just want to know that I'll be your guy. I don't want to show up and find out I'm like this sap hanging around on the outside of your life."

"I want you to come."

"Okay."

I had my suspicions, about a number of things, but promised once again that I would head out to North Carolina for the spring semester. In the meantime, I would work and save up my money.

After Eva left, I lay on the bed feeling empty.

The following night, I ended up at another club down at the beach and Tanya showed up with some of her friends. She acted really glad to see me. We went outside for a talk.

"What are you doing?" I asked her.

"Going to college. Didn't you hear?"

"No. Where?"

"UCLA."

"Oh, cool. What's your major?"

"I received an engineering scholarship."

"Wow, okay. How did that happen?"

"From studying."

"Smart ass...I never knew you were into engineering."

"You never asked."

"That's true."

We were staring out at the shore. It was black except for the bristling white surf. We could see a necklace of lights curving up the coast towards San Pedro. That trip up to the harbor and the British sailors came to mind. So did the question I had been wanting to ask Tanya.

"Have you seen Eva?" she said.

"Yeah, why? Haven't you?"

"No. We're not hanging out together anymore."

"Really? Why? What happened?"

"She's a bitch."

"To you?"

"To everybody."

I scoffed.

"I don't know about that. I know she really cared about you."

We were silent. I tossed a seashell down towards the surf. I was about to speak when Tanya beat me to it.

"There's something you should know."

I looked over

"Yeah, what?"

A couple left the club and music spilled out the door with them. Then the door closed and all was quiet again save for the murmur of the surf. I sat there waiting.

"Eva was never pregnant."

Those words hit me like a sap over the head. Never pregnant? I had been expecting to hear it was someone else's kid, not this. She was never pregnant? It made no sense.

"What do you mean, she was never pregnant?"

"Just what I said. She was never pregnant."

"So why in hell would she say that?"

"You really don't get it, do you?"

"No, I don't, so spill it."

"It was all because of Eva's parents. They told her that she had to get rid of you after the prom or she could forget about her inheritance. So Eva spent the whole trip in Europe...well, before you showed up...trying to figure out some way to scare you off. It wasn't even her idea. Beth's the one who came up with it."

"Beth?!"

"Look...I'm sorry. I'm giving you the wrong impression. None of us were thinking to hurt you. We were just sitting around Madrid one day when Eva mentioned it, and then Leslie and Beth started coming up with all these goofy ideas. You know how they are. Anyway, then Beth said, 'Hey, I know. Why don't you tell him you're pregnant'?"

"Great. I can't even believe you chicks pulled this shit on me."

"Come on, Paul. I wasn't part of it. I was just sitting in the room when all this went down."

"Yeah, well, thanks just the same."

Tanya reached out and touched my arm.

"Look, I'm sorry and I'm sure Beth and Leslie feel the same. None of us thought that Eva would actually go through with it."

"Yeah. So let me guess. The idea was, the minute I heard about Eva being pregnant, I was supposed run as fast as I could the other way."

Tanya nodded.

"She never imagined you'd come all that way, trying to rescue her."

I felt sick. To think the whole thing had been a ruse. Across the Seven Seas, playing Prince Valiant, just to be made a fool.

Then Signore Gabriele's words came back to me. A great adventure abandoned, and over some stupid girl.

"Fuck," I said.

Tanya rubbed my back.

"I'm sorry."

"Yeah, you said that."

"It got you to Europe and a great adventure."

"And I goddamned well should have stayed."

"I tried to tell you in Paris."

I nodded, realizing she was the only one who had tried.

Tanya looked my way sheepishly.

"Please don't be mad at me."

"Yeah, all right."

"It did get you to Europe. And a wonderful time."

"Yeah."

"So? What are you going to tell Eva?"

"I don't know. What *would* I tell her? Thanks for fucking me over?"

"Well, whatever you do, just don't tell her it was me."

"What do you care at this point?"

"Just don't. Please?"

"Yeah, all right...Let's go back inside. I need a drink."

That Sunday afternoon, I went to hang out with some friends at a nearby park and got to talking with a guy named Jim from my high school days. We were sitting up on a bluff, overlooking a lake and tossing pebbles down at the water.

When the subject of my recent adventures came up, Jim mentioned that his father was a pilot and that they were involved with starting a hotel down at the tip of Baja California. Jim had just returned home to organize a caravan down there by car.

"See, there are all these local roads but none of them are connected into an actual highway so we're going to try and map it out. Make it easier for people to drive down if they want to go that route."

"So that's where you're headed?"

"Yeah. It's going to be cool. Have you ever been down to Baja?"

"Ensenada. Not any farther than that."

"Yeah. You go on over the mountain from there and it's another world. People fish and farm and do whatever it takes to survive. It's like it was here a few hundred years ago. They don't even think of coming to the States. They're just living by the sun and the moon and the stars. It's a totally simple world, man."

"Yeah? Sounds far out."

"Yeah. You should come along."

"When are you leaving?"

"Tomorrow morning."

"Wow, okay."

"Yeah. We have some paperwork to deal with at the border but then we'll be heading south…So what do you think?"

"I don't know. It's kind of sudden. And I don't exactly have a lot of money."

"Hey, you'll be cool. All your food and lodging will be taken care of. All you'll need is a few bucks for drinks and stuff. Anyway, doesn't matter where we go, the universe always has a way of taking care of us."

I nodded with a smile.

"What?" Jim said.

"Oh, just…That's something I heard not too terribly long ago. While I was out on the road."

"Yeah?"

"Yeah."

I looked out across the lake with a sigh. Memories of Anastasia and Heidi and Anne and Jean had flashed through my mind while Jim was talking. So much had been left behind. So much I longed to have back. So much I wanted to go back and grab hold of and live again. And yet, if there was anything I had learned since gallivanting off to Europe, it was that life only seemed to go one way. Forward. And no matter what, life would always take care of you.

"So?" Jim said. "Did you want to come?"

I looked back at him.

"Yeah, sure. I'm always up for a new adventure."

About The Author

The product of an Irish/Italian family, Mr. Corcoran was transplanted from the clapboard New England of his youth to the cookie cutter, stucco subdivisions that increasingly littered the old ranches and disappearing orange groves south of Los Angeles in the 1960s. Ever rebellious, and true to the folk music/coffee house idealism that helped shape his early worldview, he chose to resist the Vietnam War, was a man without a country for several years and can count incarceration in a Mexican prison as one of his many colorful experiences from that era.

Having pursued a love of reading and writing in various forms all his life, Mr. Corcoran finally took that passion seriously around the turn of the millennium and has dedicated the remainder of his days to authorship. In completing the circle of destiny, he has returned to the New England of his youth and presently resides along the Rhode Island shore.

www.ingramcontent.com/pod-product-compliance
Lightning Source LLC
Chambersburg PA
CBHW021232250626
47155CB00008B/2983